OXFORD WORLD'S CLASSICS

VITA NUOVA

DANTE ALIGHIERI was born in 1265 in Florence. His family was noble but not wealthy or distinguished; his mother died when he was a child, his father before 1283. Little is known of Dante's formal education—it could have included study with the Dominicans, the Augustinians, or the Franciscans in Florence, or the university in Bologna. In his youth he fell into debt, apparently misspent some of his time with friends like Forese Donati, formed a deep friendship with the poet Guido Cavalcanti, sought learning and counsel from Brunetto Latini, and associated with a number of poets, musicians, and artists of the day. At about the age of 20 he married Gemma Donati and their union produced two sons, Pietro and Iacopo, and a daughter, Antonia. Of Beatrice, the love of Dante's life and subject of the *Vita Nuova*, not much can be verified. In 1295 Dante entered Florentine politics. In the summer of 1300 he became one of the six governing Priors of Florence. In 1301 the political situation forced Dante and his party into exile. For the rest of his life he wandered through Italy, perhaps as far away as Paris and Oxford, depending for refuge on the generosity of various nobles, performing diplomatic and legal tasks, and writing impassioned letters asking or demanding support for his ideas. He continued to write, occasionally teaching and lecturing, producing his minor works the *Convivio* and the *Monarchia*, and the great *Divina Commedia*. At some point late in life he took asylum in Ravenna where he completed the *Commedia* and died, much honoured, in 1321.

MARK MUSA holds the title of Distinguished Professor of Italian at Indiana University. He is well known for his translation of the *Divine Comedy* (Penguin Books) and other Italian classics: Petrarch, Boccaccio, Machiavelli, and the poetry of the Middle Ages, as well as Dante criticism.

D1009233

OXFORD WORLD'S CLASSICS

For over 100 years Oxford World's Classics have brought readers closer to the world's great literature. Now with over 700 titles—from the 4,000-year-old myths of Mesopotamia to the twentieth century's greatest novels—the series makes available lesser-known as well as celebrated writing.

The pocket-sized hardbacks of the early years contained introductions by Virginia Woolf, T. S. Eliot, Graham Greene, and other literary figures which enriched the experience of reading. Today the series is recognized for its fine scholarship and reliability in texts that span world literature, drama and poetry, religion, philosophy and politics. Each edition includes perceptive commentary and essential background information to meet the changing needs of readers.

OXFORD WORLD'S CLASSICS

DANTE ALIGHIERI

Vita Nuova

Translated with an Introduction and Notes by
MARK MUSA

OXFORD
UNIVERSITY PRESS

OXFORD
UNIVERSITY PRESS

Great Clarendon Street, Oxford OX2 6DP

Oxford University Press is a department of the University of Oxford.
It furthers the University's objective of excellence in research, scholarship,
and education by publishing worldwide in

Oxford New York

Athens Auckland Bangkok Bogotá Buenos Aires Calcutta
Cape Town Chennai Dar es Salaam Delhi Florence Hong Kong Istanbul
Karachi Kuala Lumpur Madrid Melbourne Mexico City Mumbai
Nairobi Paris São Paulo Singapore Taipei Tokyo Toronto Warsaw

with associated companies in Berlin Ibadan

Oxford is a registered trade mark of Oxford University Press
in the UK and in certain other countries

Published in the United States
by Oxford University Press Inc., New York

© Mark Musa 1992

The moral rights of the author have been asserted

Database right Oxford University Press (maker)

First published as a World's Classics paperback 1992
Reissued as an Oxford World's Classics paperback 1999

All rights reserved. No part of this publication may be reproduced,
stored in a retrieval system, or transmitted, in any form or by any means,
without the prior permission in writing of Oxford University Press,
or as expressly permitted by law, or under terms agreed with the appropriate
reprographics rights organizations. Enquiries concerning reproduction
outside the scope of the above should be sent to the Rights Department,
Oxford University Press, at the address above

You must not circulate this book in any other binding or cover
and you must impose this same condition on any acquirer

British Library Cataloguing in Publication Data

Data available

Library of Congress Cataloging in Publication Data
Dante Alighieri 1265–1321.
[Vita nuova. English]
Vita nuova / Dante Alighieri: translated with an introduction
by Mark Musa
p. cm.—(Oxford world's classics)
Translation of Vita nuova
Includes bibliographical references.
I. Musa, Mark. II. Title. III. Series.
PQ4315.58.M8 1992 851'.1—dc20 91–35177

ISBN 0–19–283935–7

6

Printed in Great Britain by
Clays Ltd, St Ives plc

CONTENTS

INTRODUCTION

THE *Vita nuova*, one of Dante's earliest works, is one of the first important examples of Italian literary prose. Composed sometime between 1292 and 1294, this little book is a combination of prose and poetry; many of the poems it contains were written earlier. The work may be thought of as taking shape when Dante, having arrived at a certain age (between 28 and 30), pauses to look back and examine his past experiences, both poetical and personal. Over the previous ten years (probably between 1283 and 1292) he had written many poems, but never before had he attempted to sift this body of work in order to give it order, form, or meaning.

In the opening chapter or *proemio* of his book Dante suggests the purpose of the composition he is about to undertake: he will copy from his 'book of memory' only those past experiences that belong to the period beginning his 'new life'—a life made new by the poet's first meeting with Beatrice and the Lord of Love, who, together with the poet, are the three main characters in the story. Whatever happened before his 'new life' is of no importance here, and Dante reserves the right to select from his 'book of memory' only those poems and events which he now perceives as playing a significant role in his development as a poet and his growth as a lover. His task, then, is to give meaning to that poetry which he composed and to those events which took place after his meeting with Beatrice and 'Love': this would seem to be the primary function of the prose passages in the *Vita nuova* which offer the occasion for each of the thirty-one poems in the book.

Dante, like all men, is searching for happiness, and he believes he has found it before the *Vita nuova* opens. In fact, the reason for writing the book is precisely that the poet has found his happiness, his meaning: it is his intention in this little book to reveal his discovery gradually and convincingly, as it was revealed to him. And the reader on his way through the *Vita nuova* might do well to imitate Dante's retrospective attitude: to keep looking back to the chapters he has come through to see if they have not acquired more meaning because of his journey thus far (a procedure also necessary for the reader of the *Divine Comedy*).

The book's carefully planned structure, within which there stands out in high relief each turning-point in this youthful drama of the psyche in search of a goal or final resting-place, suggests three movements—what may be called Dante's three movements in love. These are distributed as follows in the book:

> First movement   I–XVI
> Second movement   XVII–XXXI
> Third movement   XXXII–XLII.

In Chapters I–XVI are described three meetings between Dante and Beatrice on which the direction of the first movement depends: when he sees her for the first time; when she greets him for the first time; when she refuses him her greeting. After the second meeting, and also after the third, Dante has a vision in which the God of Love appears to him; the description of each vision is followed by five poems, the mood of which is inspired by the preceding vision.

Dante sees the lovely Beatrice for the first time when both of them are 9 years of age ('She appeared dressed in the most noble of colours, a subdued and decorous crimson'), and he tells us 'from that time on Love governed my soul' (Ch. II). The young Dante finds this lady 'so full of natural dignity and admirable bearing that certainly the words of the poet Homer suited her well: "She did not seem to be the daughter of any ordinary man, but rather of a god".' But it is not until 'precisely nine years' later (Ch. III) that she first greets him: 'she greeted me so miraculously that I felt I was experiencing the very summit of bliss. It was precisely the ninth hour of that day (three o'clock in the afternoon), when her sweet greeting reached me.' From that moment on throughout the first movement, Dante believes his 'bliss' to rest on his lady's greeting: in having her recognition he feels he has achieved the goal of his New Life. But then comes the third meeting (Ch. X), the day when, the poet recalls, 'the most gracious Beatrice, scourge of vice and queen of virtue, passing along a certain street, denied me her most sweet greeting in which lay all my bliss'.

When Beatrice first extends her miraculous greeting to the poet, his ecstasy is so great that he departs 'from everyone as if intoxicated' and returns to his room to enjoy, alone, the happiness of 'thinking of this most gracious lady'. His reverie turning into sweet sleep, a marvellous vision is granted him: the Lord of Love appears and utters mysterious words, only some of which the poet understands. Love appears and 'in his arms there lay a figure asleep and naked except for a crimson cloth, loosely wrapping it'. It is the lady who earlier in the day had favoured him with her greeting. Dante, unable to understand the mystifying sequence of events that follows Love's entrance, decides, once the God has departed with the lady, to make this vision the occasion for his first poem, addressing it to 'Love's faithful subjects', to the other poets of his day, requesting their help in interpreting it. But as we learn at the end of the chapter: 'The true interpretation of the dream I described was not perceived by anyone then, but now it is very clear to even the least sophisticated.' At the close of the chapter the reader shares the bewilderment that Dante and his friends experienced. The contrast made by Dante between *then* and *now* is tantalizing: we realize that we, *now*, are really back at the time of *then*: the 'then' of incomprehension. But the reader will come to share Dante's *now*: he will come to understand the vision once he reaches that point in the course of events when illumination came to Dante. Though the period following this vision is marked by the 'bliss' of Beatrice's repeated greetings, nevertheless the five sonnets that belong to this period reflect no joy; the first, as we know, recounts Dante's mysterious and terrifying vision, and the others, too, are tinged with melancholy, treating the theme of death and farewell.

After his 'blessed joy' is denied him, Dante once again (Ch. XII) closes himself in his room and, weeping, falls asleep 'like a little boy crying from a spanking'. Again the Lord of Love appears (in both visions his appearance is connected with the ninth hour), his first words being: 'My son, it is time to do away with our pretences.' During this second strange vision, Dante notices that Love is weeping, and he asks, 'Lord of all virtues, why do you weep?' And Love, shifting suddenly to Latin, replies: 'Ego tanquam centrum circuli, cui simili modo se habent circumferentie partes; tu autem non sic.' ('I am like the centre of a circle, equidistant from all points on the circumference, but you are not.') The poet, bewildered, asks, 'What is this, my Lord, that you speak so obscurely?'—only to be told by Love: 'Do not ask more than is useful to you.' The reader, too, is puzzled at this point, but he must wait patiently with Dante for the meaning to unfold.

If the first vision of Love gave the theme for the sonnet that immediately followed, it is Love himself who, in the second vision, suggests to the poet the theme for his next composition: a plea to the Lady Beatrice for mercy. The sonnets that follow this ballad describe the strange and powerful and contradictory effects of love on the poet. At this point it may be well to note that among the many poets who answered Dante's first sonnet was Guido Cavalcanti, referred to as 'my first friend' ('My sending the sonnet to him resulted in the forming of our friendship'). And it is perhaps not without significance that Dante mentions his 'first friend' in the opening section of his book, for when he treats of love in this first movement, it is from the point of view adopted by Cavalcanti throughout his own *canzoniere*: no poet had investigated more thoroughly and successfully the dramatic and mysterious possibilities of love or its manifold effects on the lover. It is as though Dante had assigned himself a guide for the first phase of his journey, particularly for the closing self-analytical sonnets in which he probes into the workings of love on the human heart.

He can do this at last because of the second appearance of Love, who has encouraged him to open his heart to his

lady. It is this unfolding of the inner self, the open investigation of his sad condition as a lover, that enables the poet
to suspect that he has been moving in the wrong direction.
In Chapter XVII he decides to abandon the vein of sad
self-analysis in order 'to take up a new theme, one more
lofty than the last', and in Chapter XVIII, which treats the
occasion for his new theme, Dante has fully realized that
his earlier 'bliss' which turned to grief was made of unsub-
stantial stuff: true happiness cannot come from something
as arbitrary and changeable as the greeting of his lady. This
greeting, which once, he admits, 'was the end of all my
desires', is replaced by a new goal, one that cannot fail him:
his 'bliss' will rest in those words that praise her; from now
on, looking beyond himself, he will dedicate his poetic
efforts to exalting his gracious lady. And in Chapter XIX
he initiates his programme for the second movement with
the *canzone* 'Ladies, refined and sensitive in Love, | I wish
to speak with you about my lady.' The poetic framework of
this new movement is constituted by three *canzoni* which
enclose eight shorter poems: the central *canzone* of the triad,
which stands at the centre of the book itself (being the
sixteenth poem in a sequence of thirty-one), is separated
from the first *canzone* by four sonnets and from the third
by three sonnets and an imperfect *canzone*.

In the first sonnet of this new movement ('Love and the
gracious heart are but one thing') Dante considers the
mysterious origin of love and pays tribute to another dear
friend, to whom he refers in the second verse of the poem
as 'il saggio'. This 'sage' is Guido Guinizzelli of Bologna,
another distinguished poet of Dante's time, referred to by
Dante in the *Divine Comedy* as 'father of me and of my
betters, all who wrote a sweet and graceful poetry of love'
(*Purgatory*, xxvi, lines 97–9). In his own verse Guinizzelli
devotes himself mainly to the praise of his lady, her great
worth, her angelic and miraculous qualities; he, therefore,
is the expert in this new realm just as Guido Cavalcanti was
in the realm of the psychological effects of love. Guinizzelli,
then, might be thought of as Dante's new guide for his
second movement in love.

After a sonnet in praise of his lady (Ch. XXI), 'The power of Love borne in my lady's eyes', Dante tells us in the following chapter that Beatrice's father has died. This serves as the occasion for the next two sonnets: the theme of death, which was the main theme of the first five poems in the book, returns as we approach the centre of the *Vita nuova*.

In Chapter XXIII Dante tells of an illness that overtook him and caused him 'to suffer intense pain constantly for nine days'; in one of the longest and most beautiful prose passages in the *Vita nuova* he recounts a terrible dream he had 'on the ninth day' of his illness. After his dream he decides to compose a *canzone* ('A very young and sympathetic lady') in which he will tell those gentle ladies, who attended him during his illness and offered him comfort when he awoke from his dream, what happened in his 'false imaginings'. He dreams that Beatrice dies. But this dream, which foreshadows the actual death of Beatrice, is only one in a series of portents pointing to her death: having arrived at this point, the reader will remember other 'intimations of mortality' interspersed within the work (the earlier sonnets treating death and separation). Indeed, if he reads carefully this remarkable *canzone* and pauses to seek *now* for meaning that was not clear *then*, he will find himself turning back to the account of the first vision of Love (who is holding the body of Beatrice in his arms). The significance of this first vision 'was not perceived by anyone then, but now it is very clear to even the least sophisticated'.

Let the reader also return to Chapter XII, where for the second time the Lord of Love appeared to his vassal and, when asked by Dante why he wept, pronounced the mysterious words: 'I am like the centre of a circle, equidistant from all points on the circumference, but you are not.' Dante, finding these words obscure, had asked for further explanation, only to be told by Love: 'Do not ask more than is useful to you': Love was withholding something from his vassal. But now, in this central *canzone*, Love tells him (and these are the only words Love speaks): 'I'll not hide a thing from you; come now to see our lady lying dead.' This brief announcement justifies Love's simile in Chapter XII: this god being like the centre of a circle, he was able to see all points on the circumference of time: not only the past and present but also the future, the death of Beatrice; Dante, as Love reminded him, had no such omniscience. But the fact that Dante has been vouchsafed in his dream a non-ambiguous vision of the future, that he has been allowed to share for a moment the god's clairvoyance, is surely a sign of the spiritual growth that the poet by now has achieved.

The vivid description of Beatrice's passing is given in the central *canzone* recounting Dante's dream. As the reader will soon see, this is the only description of her death that the book contains: the event itself, when it occurs, is reported with no detail. Because of this fact, and because the dream in question is, in truth, a vision of reality, it could be said that Beatrice dies at the centre of the *Vita nuova*—a symmetrical detail of utmost significance, since her death is the most important event in the poet's spiritual biography: the irradiating centre of his New Life.

After the dramatic account of Beatrice's death, the poet in the following four sonnets returns to praising his lady, who, in fact, is still alive. In these sonnets, however, Beatrice appears as one who has already ascended to heaven and who is allowed through the goodness of God to return to earth for the benefit of all mankind. In the opening prose section of Chapter XXVI, which presents the occasion for Dante's famous sonnet, 'Such sweet decorum and such gentle graces', we see not only that Beatrice appears more miraculous to Dante but that even the townsfolk seem to sense her uniqueness: 'This most gracious lady of whom I have spoken in the preceding poems came into such widespread favour among the people that when she walked down a street, people ran to see her.' And in the sonnet she

> . . . seems a creature come from heaven to earth,
> a miracle manifest in reality.

Then in the following sonnet we read:

> all those who keep her company must give
> their thanks to God for such sweet grace as this.

Recollections of the poet's first introspective movement in

love appear in the fourth poem, which begins:

> So long a time has Love kept me a slave
> and in his lordship fully seasoned me,
> that even though at first I felt him harsh,
> now tender is his power in my heart.

With this imperfect *canzone* it is as though the poet, approaching the end of his second movement, were looking back to his first stage in an attempt to give meaning to all that has happened to him thus far in his 'New Life'.

In Chapter XXVIII, with calm and dignity, Dante announces the death of Beatrice (she is called to glory by the 'God of Justice' at the moment the poet is composing a *canzone*); he accepts the death of his gracious lady without astonishment, as though it were an event long past, and the reader must also accept it without amazement, for, certainly, he has been more than adequately prepared for the passing away of Beatrice. Although Dante says that he will not discuss her departure, for it was not intended in 'this little book', he does tell us at the beginning of the next chapter that 'her most worthy soul departed during the first hour of the ninth day of the month'.

Musing on other possible relationships between Beatrice's life and the number nine (and at this point the reader will remember that the first two visions occur in connection with the ninth hour; and that Dante's first meeting with Beatrice takes place when both are in their ninth year, their second meeting occurring nine years later), Dante concludes that 'she and this number are actually synonymous' and 'if three is the sole factor of nine and the sole factor of miracles is three, that is, Father, Son, and Holy Ghost, who are three in One, then this lady is accompanied by the number nine so that it may be understood that she was a nine, or a miracle, whose root, namely of the miracle, is the miraculous Trinity itself.'

Dante's meaning is unmistakable: Beatrice is a miracle and she is like Christ (let the reader look back into the preceding twenty-eight chapters to assure himself that he has been well prepared for such an analogy): she comes from heaven to earth, takes on flesh, dies, and ascends into heaven (to save the soul of Dante). Having shown Beatrice as a miracle, especially in the poetry of this central portion of his book, and having devoted a chapter to a discussion of the number nine in order to prove that she is truly a miracle and like the Trinity, Dante is ready to progress into the third and final movement in love. By now the new direction the poet must take has been made evident by Beatrice's death: he must move upward toward where his lady rests, for it is there that he must find his true 'bliss': there is his final and imperishable goal.

But the poet finds it difficult to move upward, because he is no longer guided by the physical presence of Beatrice, whom he had loved as a woman of flesh and blood. The reader will observe that much of the self-pity and general concern with self which dominated the first movement returns in the opening poems of this last movement to impede the poet's progress; indeed, the third *canzone*, which concludes the second movement, opens on such a note: 'The eyes grieving through pity for the heart . . .'. It is true that in this lament for Beatrice, the new direction is predicated ('Beatrice has ascended to high heaven'): the theme is introduced that will come to predominate in the final movement. But here, what might have been the joy of 'high heaven' is overshadowed by grief that Beatrice is gone. And Dante, left behind on earth with only his sorrow for company, appears unable, in himself, to begin the upward movement to his true goal. This can come about only when after much suffering, and much struggling with the problem of Beatrice's departure, the poet is brought to see, by a painful experience, the insidious dangers of self-pity.

The first sonnet of the new movement is written, Dante tells us, at the request of a friend 'second after my first friend'. The reader will remember that Dante's first friend, the poet Cavalcanti, was mentioned after the opening sonnet of the *Vita nuova* and that in the first sonnet of the second movement tribute was paid to another friend and poet, Guido Guinizzelli—the two movements reflecting much of the tone and themes of the two poets who had guided

Dante's first literary endeavours. But for this third movement there could be no poetic guide: here Dante will go beyond Cavalcanti and Guinizzelli and all other poets of his day: not so much in tone or theme (concern with self as Love's sufferer is still present through much of the movement) as in direction: no other poet had exalted and idealized his lady to the extent that Dante does. It is then no man of letters to whom Dante is referring as his second friend, but simply a close relative of Beatrice—who asks the poet to write something for him about 'a lady who was dead'.

Dante, who immediately understands the allusion, writes two poems (one a sonnet, the other an incomplete *canzone*) of lament for the death of Beatrice. The first is inspired by self-pity alone; the second, in which the poet calls upon Death to take him, opens on the same note, though the last lines do vaguely suggest the new direction.

> This is because the pleasure of her beauty,
> having removed itself from mortal sight,
> was transformed into beauty of the soul
> spreading throughout the heavens
> a light of love that greets the angels there,
> and moves their keen and lofty intellects
> to marvel at such graciousness up there.

But Dante, it would seem, is still too overtaken by his great loss to hear and understand his own weeping.

In Chapter XXXIV Dante, one year after the death of Beatrice, composes a sonnet ('in the form of an anniversary poem') which has two beginnings—thereby reflecting the struggle of the psyche with the two conflicting themes of this movement. The first beginning, in which Dante succeeds in transcending his suffering, is in the new direction:

> The gracious lady came into my mind,
> the lady who because of her great worth
> was placed by His most lofty Majesty
> in that calm realm of heaven where Mary is.

Unable, however, to sustain this attitude, the poet begins anew with the words:

> That gracious lady came into my mind,
> that lady for whom Love is weeping still,

and this motif of tears continues through the poem.

After his abortive attempt to conquer his melancholy, Dante finds temporary consolation in the compassion that is offered him by a stranger: 'a gracious lady, young and very beautiful' (as he tells us in Chapter XXXV); 'it seemed all pity was concentrated in her'. He composes a sonnet, and then another in the following chapter, both in praise of this compassionate young lady. These are followed by two other sonnets: in the first the poet, who is angry with himself for falling in love, presents an interior dialogue in which the heart or Reason curses the eyes for roving; in the second (after the 'battle of the thoughts' in the prose section), Desire sweetly attempts to persuade Reason in favour of the new lady.

But Desire, 'this adversary of reason', is worsted by a vision that comes to the poet. As he tells us in the beginning of Chapter XXXIX ('One day about the hour of nones . . .'), his imagination shows him Beatrice, clothed in crimson garments as in their first meeting; and Dante says, 'she seemed young, of the same age as when I first saw her'. This vision causes him to think deeply about her, to look back and re-examine his New Life in the hope of finding a way to free himself from his need for pity in order to be able to move toward happiness. And it is precisely by means of this looking back, 'and remembering her [Beatrice] in the sequence of past times'—a very specialized and important way of looking back—that the poet is able to liberate himself from self-pity and from that lady who was herself Pity incarnate: 'Then I began to think about her, and remembering her in the sequence of past times, my heart began remorsefully to repent of the desire by which it had so unworthily let itself be possessed for some time contrary to firm reason; and once I had rejected this evil desire, all my thoughts turned back to their most gracious Beatrice.'

From this time on, the poet's thoughts are dedicated exclusively to Beatrice: what fills his heart is 'the name of that most gracious one and how she departed from us'. Certainly to remember Beatrice in the sequence of past events, and especially 'how she departed from us' (a departure so similar to the way the Son of God left this earth to ascend into heaven), will be Dante's means of salvation, for Beatrice clearly points to God. In the course of his three movements in Love Dante learns that true happiness, which is the goal of all men, lies above and beyond the material world, and that only by experience, failure, and continuous struggle for meaning and understanding, which is the movement of the *Vita nuova*, can man hope to attain his goal.

In the first of the last three sonnets the remorseful poet, as if to purge himself, lays bare his shame for having let his eyes wander in the wrong direction. The sonnet ends: 'and many words relating to her death'; Dante will never again allow himself to forget the significance of 'how she departed from us'.

In the prose of the following chapter (XL) we are told of some pilgrims who were passing through 'the middle of the city where the most gracious lady was born, lived, and died' on a pilgrimage 'to see the blessed image that Jesus Christ left us as a copy of His most beautiful face'; this is followed by a sonnet in which Dante pretends to speak to the pilgrims about this city's great loss. Though this, like the preceding sonnet, is a lament for the loss of Beatrice, both are lacking in self-pity; they serve to prepare the way for the closing sonnet, which the poet refers to as 'something new'.

Having received word from two 'worthy ladies' that they desire to see some of his poetry, Dante decides not only to send them several of his compositions but also to write 'something new' to accompany them. This request on the part of these two ladies should invite the reader to recall another request of some other 'worthy ladies' in Chapter XVIII: 'We beg you to tell us wherein this bliss of yours now lies', to which Dante replies: 'In those words that praise my lady.' And now in sending the ladies his 'something new', the poet is again telling them where his happiness now lies: above, in heaven, with Beatrice:

Beyond the sphere that makes the widest round,
    passes the sigh which issues from my heart;
    a strange, new understanding that sad Love
    imparts to it keeps urging it on high.
When it has reached the place of its desiring,
    it sees a lady held in reverence,
    splendid in light, and through her radiance
    the pilgrim spirit gazes at her being.
But when it tries to tell me what it saw,
    I cannot understand the subtle words
    it speaks to the sad heart that makes it speak.
    I know it talks of that most gracious one,
    because it often mentions Beatrice;
    this much is very clear to me, dear ladies.

In the poet's prose analysis of this sonnet he tells us that he calls his a 'pilgrim spirit' because 'it makes the journey up there spiritually and remains there like a pilgrim far from home'. Perhaps this 'pilgrim spirit' that travels 'beyond the sphere' to gaze on Beatrice should remind us of those pilgrims mentioned in the preceding chapter who were on their way to look upon 'the blessed image that Jesus Christ left us'. Again and again Beatrice is presented as a reflection of Christ.

    In this, the final sonnet of the *Vita nuova*, it is the poet's sigh which travels 'Beyond the sphere that makes the widest round' to see his lady who is 'held in reverence'; in the *Divine Comedy* the poet himself, again in three movements, will make the journey beyond the same sphere, and the same gracious and glorious lady of the *Vita nuova*, who died to point the way beyond, will, in the third and final movement of the *Divine Comedy*, live again to guide her pilgrim lover beyond the spheres to God.

    The short prose chapter which brings the book to a close speaks of a miraculous vision enjoyed by Dante, which enables him to announce the coming of the *Divine Comedy* and the important role Beatrice will have in it: 'if it be the wish of Him through whom all things flourish, that my life continue for a few more years, I hope to write of her that which has never been written of any other woman'.

The distribution of the thirty-one poems of the *Vita nuova*, of which the three *canzoni* (represented below by Roman numerals) form the major compositions, may be illustrated by the following simple schema, which shows the tripartite construction of the book and the central position of the death of Beatrice, who (in death as in life) determined the direction of Dante's movements in love:

10 I 4 II 4 III 10.

But if examined more closely, the structure of the book will show, still more clearly, how the distribution of the poetic compositions serves to underline the significance of Beatrice as the overall poetic theme of the work. To perceive this we need only subdivide the four groups of shorter poems (10–4–4–10) according to one consistent principle; in each, one poem distinguishes itself clearly from the others in its group.

Of the ten poems of the first movement, it is the first that stands apart from all the rest: the introductory nature of the opening sonnet, which is addressed to 'all Love's faithful subjects', is obvious. Similarly in the second movement we must set aside the opening sonnet of the first group of four, which deals with love in a general way, reaffirming Guinizzelli's theory of 'Love and the gracious heart'. In contrast, those that follow treat of Beatrice herself (and serve to prepare the way for her strange and miraculous death in the *canzone* that follows). In the second group of four poems it is the last that must be distinguished from those that precede: while these sonnets are devoted exclusively to praise of 'madonna', the fourth poem (which is not a sonnet but an imperfect *canzone*) serves to summarize the poet's condition ever since he has been in the service of Love. Finally, in the third movement or second group of ten poems, the last, which Dante himself has offered as 'something new' and which represents the poet's pilgrim spirit as gazing upon Beatrice in heaven, must stand in isolation as a glorious climax: a climax of the *Vita nuova* and a prelude to the *Divine Comedy*.

If now we modify the schema offered above to take

account of the subdivisions just indicated, we see how the numbers, thus rearranged, bear witness to the significance of Beatrice:

$$1—9 \text{ I } 1—3 \longleftrightarrow \text{ II } \longleftrightarrow 3—1 \text{ III } 9—1.$$

The importance of the numbers 1, 3, and 9 has long since become clear to the reader: Beatrice, who is one person, is always associated with 'nine' ('she and this number are actually synonymous') so that all may understand that she is a miracle whose root is the miraculous Trinity. At the same time, as the arrows indicate, the distribution makes still clearer the pivotal position of the central *canzone*: the poem looks forward to and back upon the death of Beatrice. It could be said that the *Vita nuova* begins in the middle in the sense that the meaning of the whole stems from its centre.

It is as though Love were speaking once again: 'Ego tanquam centrum circuli, cui simili modo se habent circumferentie partes'.

NOTE ON THE TRANSLATION

IN this translation of the *Vita nuova*, I have avoided the use of rhyme in the poetry, continuing to render the Italian original in English blank verse. My reasons for not submitting to the tyranny of rhyme in translating Dante's poetry have been presented in the Introduction to my translation of the *Divine Comedy* (vol. i: *Inferno*, Penguin Classics, pp. 57–64). There I also expressed my ideas about what faithfulness to the original should mean for the translator of poetry.

It might seem that the problem would be much less difficult for the translator of prose. I should say that, although it is less complicated, it is, none the less, difficult if the original text was composed centuries ago, when the patterns of prose style were quite different from those of our own time. There is no doubt about it: to the reader who goes from modern Italian prose to the prose of the *Vita nuova* the older style seems stilted and verbose; and the reader always seems to be in the midst of a dependent clause, or to have just escaped from one, or to be about to enter into another. Yet it would be a sacrilege to reduce Dante's elaborate prose periods to simpler predications. On the other hand, should one offer the reader a translation with sentences that may be tedious to read, and language which will strike him as unnatural? To find a happy compromise is not easy, and this is particularly true of the narrative prose of the *Vita nuova*. The suggestion of 'stuffiness' that would be unavoidable in a translation of a philosophical work such as Dante's *Convivio* would certainly be tolerated by all readers, and perhaps even enjoyed. It is less enjoyable in a narrative; and Dante's narrative style is at times indistinguishable from the expository style of his *Convivio*. Thus, in Chapter XXII of the *Vita nuova*, after announcing the death of Beatrice's father, he continues:

Since such a departure is sorrowful to those who remain and who have been friends of the deceased; and since there is no friendship more intimate than that of a good father for a good child, or of a good child for a good father; . . . and since her father, as is believed by many and it is the truth, was exceedingly good—then it is clear that this lady was bitterly filled with sorrow.

Sometimes, it is true, careful study will reveal that what seems at first glance to be unpardonable pedantry was inspired by the deepest artistry. But many times the explanation for Dante's stylistic choices must be sought in certain very personal predilections of the author which are generally not shared by writers of narrative. Surely whatever it was that inspired the author of the *Vita nuova* to attach to most of his poems a minutely precise explanation of their content—thereby anticipating, though for a different purpose, his procedure in the *Convivio*—helps explain the choice of his prose style in general.

If the reader believes, as he must, that Dante's prose style, more appropriate to exposition than to narrative, represents a deliberate choice by a man of genius, he will probably appreciate the goal I have set myself: to respect every detail of Dante's sentence structure as far as it is possible to do so within the limits set by the patterns of English idiom.

SELECT BIBLIOGRAPHY

Bigongiari, Dino, 'Dante's *Vita nuova*', *Essays on Dante and Medieval Culture* (Florence: Olschki, 1964), 65–76.

Corsi, Sergio, *Il 'modus digressivus' nella* Divina Commedia (Potomac, Md.: Scripta Humanistica, 1987).

Cro, Stelio, '*Vita Nuova* figura *Comoediae*: Dante tra la Villana Morte e Matelda', *Italian Culture*, 6 (1985), 13–30.

D'Andrea, Antonio, 'La struttura della *Vita Nuova*: Le divisioni delle rime', *Yearbook of Italian Studies*, 4 (1980), 13–40.

De Bonfils Templer, Margherita, *Itinerario di Amore: Dialettica di Amore e Morte nella* Vita nuova (Chapel Hill, NC: U. of North Carolina Studies in Romance Languages and Literatures, 1973).

De Robertis, Domenico (ed.), *Vita nuova* (Milan and Naples: Riccardo Ricciardi, 1980).

—— *Il libro della* Vita Nuova (2nd edn.; Florence: Sansoni, 1970).

Elata-Aster, Gerda, 'Gathering the Leaves and Squaring the Circle: *Recording*, *Reading* and *Writing* in Dante's *Vita Nuova* and *Divina Commedia*', *Italian Quarterly*, 24: 92 (1983), 5–26.

Fletcher, Jefferson Butler, 'The "True Meaning" of Dante's *Vita nuova*', *Romanic Review*, 11 (1920), 95–148.

Guzzardo, John, 'Number Symbolism in the *Vita Nuova*', *Canadian Journal of Italian Studies*, 8: 30 (1985), 12–31.

Harrison, Robert Pogue, *The Body of Beatrice* (Baltimore, Md.: Johns Hopkins UP, 1988).

Hollander, Robert, '*Vita Nuova*: Dante's Perceptions of Beatrice', *Dante Studies*, 92 (1974), 1–18.

Holloway, Julia Bolton, 'The *Vita Nuova*: Paradigms of Pilgrimage', *Dante Studies*, 103 (1985), 103–24.

Howe, Kay, 'Dante's Beatrice: The Nine and the Ten', *Italica*, 52 (1975), 364–71.

Klemp, P. J., 'The Woman in the Middle: Layers of Love in Dante's *Vita Nuova*', *Italica*, 61: 3 (1984), 185–94.

Lora, Francesco, *Nuova interpretazione della* Vita nuova (Naples: Francesco Perrella (Società Anonima Editrice), 1918).

McKenzie, Kenneth, 'The Symbolic Structure of Dante's *Vita Nuova*', *PMLA* 18 (1903), 341–55.

Mazzaro, Jerome, *The Figure of Dante: An Essay on the* Vita Nuova (Princeton, NJ: Princeton UP, 1981).

Mazzotta, Giuseppe, 'The Language of Poetry in the *Vita Nuova*', *Rivista di studi italiani*, 1: 1 (1983), 3–14.

Musa, Mark, *Dante's* Vita Nuova: *A Translation and an Essay* (Bloomington: Indiana UP, 1973).

Nolan, Barbara, 'The *Vita Nuova*: Dante's Book of Revelation', *Dante Studies*, 88 (1970), 51–77.

Norton, Charles Eliot, *The New Life of Dante Alighieri* (Boston and New York: Houghton-Mifflin, 1895).

Pipa, Arshi, 'Personaggi della *Vita Nuova*: Dante, Cavalcanti e la famiglia Portinari', *Italica*, 62: 2 (1985), 99–115.

Scott, J. A., 'Dante's "Sweet New Style" and the *Vita Nuova*', *Italica*, 42 (1965), 98–107.

Shaw, J. E., 'Ego tamquam centrum circuli: *Vita Nuova* XII', *Italica*, 24 (1947), 113–18.

Singleton, Charles S., *An Essay on the* Vita Nuova (Cambridge, Mass: Harvard UP, 1958).

Smarr, Janet Levarie, 'Celestial Patterns and Symmetries in the *Vita Nuova*', *Dante Studies*, 98 (1980), 145–50.

Sturm-Maddox, Sarah, 'The Pattern of Witness: Narrative Design in the *Vita Nuova*', *Forum Italicum*, 12: 2 (1978), 216–32.

Trovato, Mario, 'Il capitolo xii della *Vita Nuova*', *Forum Italicum*, 16: 1–2 (1982), 19–32.

Vincent, E. R., 'The Crisis in the *Vita Nuova*', *Century Essays on Dante by Members of the Oxford Dante Society* (Oxford: Clarendon Press, 1965), 132–42.

A CHRONOLOGY OF
DANTE ALIGHIERI

1265   Dante Alighieri is born in Florence.

1266   Representative democracy restored in Florence with the establishment of the Second Republic.

1270–73 Death of Dante's mother, Donna Bella (Gabriella).

1283?   Death of his father, Alighiero.

1285?   Dante's marriage to Gemma Donati, to whom he was betrothed in 1277.

1289   The battles of Campaldino and Caprona, in which Dante may have participated.

1290   Dante enters a period of philosophic study; he writes his 'stony rhymes' (*Rime petrose*) during the next decade.

1293–94 Compiles the *Vita Nuova*.

1294   Boniface VIII crowned Pope.

1300   Jubilee Year; Dante elected one of the six priors of Florence.

1301   Travels to Rome; Charles of Valois enters Florence.

1302   Black Guelfs take control of Florence; Dante condemned to death by burning with confiscation of all his goods; he goes into exile.

1307   *De vulgari eloquentia*, a treatise on language, and the *Convivio*, a compendium of wisdom, interrupted by the undertaking of the *Divina Commedia*.

1309   Pope Clement V establishes the papacy in Avignon.

1310   Henry VII, Emperor, enters Italy; Dante writes three Latin epistles in favour of union of Church and State.

1313   Henry VII dies 21 August at Buonconvento.

1314–15 Dante finishes the *Inferno* and the *Purgatorio* at the court of Cangrande della Scala in Verona.

1315   Refuses amnesty as dishonourable; his death sentence extended to his sons.

1317?   Completes the *Monarchia*, a defence of the Emperor.

1318?   Moves to the court of Guido Novella da Polenta, nephew of Francesca da Rimini, in Ravenna.

1319–20 Declines poet laureateship of Bologna.

1321   Dies in September in Ravenna, after a diplomatic journey to Venice.

        The *Paradiso*, dedicated to Cangrande, made public posthumously.

Vita Nuova

I

IN that part of the book of my memory before which there would be little to read is found a chapter heading which says: 'Here begins a new life'.* It is my intention to copy into this little book the words I find written under that heading—if not all of them, at least their significance.

II

NINE times already since my birth the heaven of light* had
circled back to almost the same point when the now glorious
lady of my mind first appeared to my eyes. She was called
Beatrice by many who could not have possibly called her
by any other name. She had been in this life long enough
to allow the starry heavens to move a twelfth of a degree*
to the east in her time; that is, she appeared to me almost
in the beginning of her ninth year, and I first saw her near
the end of my ninth year. She appeared dressed in the most
noble of colours, a subdued and decorous crimson, girded
and adorned in a style suitable to her years. At that moment,
and what I say is true, the vital spirit,* the one that dwells
in the most secret chamber of the heart, began to tremble
so violently that even the least pulses of my body were
strangely affected; and trembling, it spoke these words:
'Here is a god stronger than I, who shall come to rule over
me.'* At that point the animal spirit, the one abiding in the
high chamber to which all the senses bring their perceptions,
was stricken with amazement, and speaking directly to the
spirits of sight,* said these words: 'Now your bliss has
appeared.'* At that moment the natural spirit, the one which
dwells in that part where our nourishment is attended to,
began to weep, and weeping, said these words: 'Alas, wretch
that I am, from now on I shall be hindered often.'* Let me
say that from that time on Love governed my soul, which
became so readily betrothed to him and over which he
reigned with such assurance and lordship given him through
the power of my imagination that it became necessary for
me to tend to his every pleasure. Often he commanded me
to seek this youngest of angels; and therefore I went in
search of her many times in my youth and found her so
full of natural dignity and admirable bearing that certainly
the words of the poet Homer suited her well: 'She did not

seem to be the daughter of any ordinary man, but rather of a god.'* And though her image, which remained constantly with me, was Love's assurance of holding me, it was of such a pure quality that never did it permit me to be ruled by Love without the trusted counsel of reason (dealing in those things wherein such advice would profitably be heeded). Since to dwell too long on the passions and actions of my early years may appear frivolous, I shall leave them, and omitting many things which could be copied from my book of memory whence these derived, I turn to those words which are written in my mind under more important headings.

III

AFTER so many days had passed that precisely nine years had been completed since the appearance I have just described of this very gracious lady, it happened that on the last day of this nine-year period the blessed lady appeared to me dressed in pure white standing between two ladies of high bearing both older than herself. While walking down a street, she turned her eyes to where I was standing faint-hearted and, with that indescribable graciousness that today is rewarded in the eternal life, she greeted me so miraculously that I felt I was experiencing the very summit of bliss. It was precisely the ninth hour* of that day (three o'clock in the afternoon), when her sweet greeting reached me. And since that was the first time her words had entered my ears, I was so overcome with ecstasy that I departed from everyone as if intoxicated. I returned to the loneliness of my room and began thinking of this most gracious lady. In my reverie a sweet sleep seized me, and a marvellous vision* appeared to me. I seemed to see a cloud the colour of fire in my room and in that cloud a lordly man, frightening to behold, yet apparently marvellously filled with joy. He said many things of which I understood only a few; among them was, 'I am your master.'* It seemed to me that in his arms there lay a figure asleep and naked except for a crimson cloth loosely wrapping it. Looking at it very intently, I realized that it was the lady of the blessed greeting, the lady who earlier in the day had favoured me with her salutation. In one of his hands he held a fiery object, and he seemed to say these words: 'Behold your heart.'* And after a short while, he seemed to awaken the sleeping one, and through the power of his art made her eat this burning object in his hand. Hesitantly, she ate it.

It was only a short while after this that his happiness turned into bitterest weeping, and weeping, he folded his arms around this lady and together they seemed to ascend towards the heavens. I felt such anguish at their departure that my sleep could not endure; it was broken and I awakened. At once I began to reflect, and I realized that the vision had appeared to me in the fourth hour of the night;* that is, it was without a doubt the first of the last nine hours of the night. Musing on what I had seen, I decided to make it known to many of the famous poets* of the times. Since recently I had discovered my abilities as a poet, I resolved to compose a sonnet in which I would address all Love's faithful subjects; and requesting them to interpret my vision, I wrote to them everything that I had seen in my sleep. Then I began this sonnet* which begins: 'To every loving heart'.

> To every loving heart and captive soul
>   into whose sight these present words may come
>   for some elucidation in reply,
>   greetings I bring for their sweet lord's sake,* Love.
> The first three hours of night were almost spent,
>   the time that every star shines down on us,
>   when Love appeared to me all of a sudden,
>   and I still shudder at the memory.
> Joyous Love looked to me while he was holding
>   my heart within his hands, and in his arms
>   my lady lay asleep wrapped in a veil.
>   He woke her then and trembling and obedient
>   she ate that burning heart out of his hand;
>   weeping I saw him then depart from me.

This sonnet is divided into two parts. In the first part I extend greetings and ask for an answer, while in the second I signify what requires an answer. The second part begins: 'The first three hours'.

This sonnet was answered by many possessing a variety of opinions, among whom was the one I call my first friend,* who composed a sonnet which begins: 'I think that you beheld all worth.' My sending the sonnet to him resulted in the forming of our friendship. The true interpretation of the dream I described was not perceived by anyone then, but now it is very clear to even the least sophisticated.

IV

AFTER that vision my natural spirit began to slacken in its working for I had become wholly absorbed in the thought of this most gracious lady. It was but a short time before I became so weak and so frail that many of my friends were concerned about my appearance; others, full of envy, were striving to learn about me that which above all I wished to keep secret.* Then I, becoming aware of the maliciousness of their questions, by Love's will, which commanded me according to the counsel of reason, would answer by saying that it was Love that had governed me so. I said that it was Love because on my face so many of his signs were clearly marked that they were impossible to conceal. And when people would ask, 'For whom has Love so undone you?' I, smiling, would look at them and say nothing.

V

ONE day it happened that this most gracious of ladies was sitting in a place where words about the queen of glory* were heard, and I was in a place from which I could behold my bliss. Between her and me, in direct line with my vision, sat a worthy lady of very pleasing aspect who gazed at me frequently as if amazed at my glances which appeared to be directed at her. And many became aware of her gazing at me, and such note was taken of it that as I left this place I heard someone near me say: 'See how that man is utterly consumed for the sake of that lady'; and as they named the lady, I realized they were speaking of the one who had been in direct line between the most gracious Beatrice and my gaze. Then I was much relieved, assuring myself that my glances had not revealed my secret to others that day. At once I thought of making this good lady a screen for the truth,* and so well did I play my part that in a short time my secret was believed known by most of those who talked about me. Thanks to this lady, I found protection for several years and months, and in order to strengthen people's false belief, I wrote certain trifles for her in verse which I have no intention of including here except in so far as doing so might serve to treat of that most gracious Beatrice; therefore, I will omit them all except for a few things that are clearly in praise of the latter.

VI

MOREOVER, during the time that this lady acted as a screen for so great a love on my part, a desire possessed me to record the name of that most gracious Beatrice and to accompany it with the names of many other ladies and especially with the name of this worthy lady. I took the names of sixty of the most beautiful women of the city in which my lady had been placed by the Almighty and composed an epistle in the form of a *serventese** which I shall not include here. In fact, I would not have mentioned it, had it not been that while composing the list, it miraculously happened that the name of my lady appeared as the ninth among the names of those ladies, as if refusing to appear beside any other number.

VII

IT became necessary for the lady who had so long helped me conceal my true feelings to leave the aforementioned city and to journey to a distant town; wherefore I, bewildered by the fact that my ideal defence now had failed me, became very dejected, more so than I myself would have previously believed possible. And knowing that if I were not to lament her departure somewhat, people would the sooner become aware of my secret, I decided to write a few grieving words in the form of a sonnet, which I shall include here because my lady was the immediate occasion for many of its words, as is evident to one who understands. Then I devised this sonnet* which begins: 'O you who travel'.

O you who travel on the road of Love,
    pause here and look about
    for any man whose grief surpasses mine.*
I ask this only: hear me out, then judge
    if I am not indeed
    of every torment keeper and abode.
Love, surely not for my slight worthiness,
    but through his nobleness,
Once gave me so serene and sweet a life
that many times I heard it said of me,
    'Lord, what great qualities
    give this man's heart the richness of such joy?'
Now all is spent of that first wealth of joy
    that sprang to birth from Love's bright treasury;
    I live in poverty,
    in writing's place comes insecurity.
And therefore I have sought to be like those
    who cover up their poverty for shame:
    I dress in happiness
    but in my heart I weep and waste away.

There are two principal parts to this sonnet. In the first part my intent is to call upon Love's faithful through the words of the prophet Jeremiah, 'All ye who pass by, behold and see if there be any sorrow like unto my sorrow',* and to beg that they deign to hear me. In the second part I tell of the position in which Love had placed me, with a meaning other than that expressed in the beginning and ending of the sonnet, and I tell what I have lost. The second part begins: 'Love, surely not'.

VIII

AFTER the departure of this worthy lady it pleased the Lord of angels to call to his glory a young lady of exceedingly kind aspect, loved and admired in the aforementioned city. I saw her body lying lifeless in the midst of many ladies* who were weeping most pitifully. Then, remembering that I had formerly seen her in the company of that very gracious lady, I could not hold back my tears; and weeping, I resolved to say something about her death, in recognition of having seen her sometimes with my lady. And I touch upon this in the latter part of the verses concerning this matter, as will be evident to the discerning. Then I devised these two sonnets, the first beginning: 'If Love', and the second: 'Brute death'.

> If Love himself weep, shall not lovers weep,
>   hearing for what sad cause he pours his tears?
> Love hears his ladies crying their distress,
>   showing forth bitter sorrow through their eyes
> to grieve how villainous death in gentle hearts
>   has worked his cruel and all-destroying arts,
> and laid waste all that earth could find to praise
>   in gentle lady save sweet chastity.*
> Hear then how Love paid homage to this lady:
>   in human form I saw him weeping there
>   beside the stilled, fair image of her grace;
> and often he would raise his eyes toward heaven
>   where that sweet soul already had its seat
>   which once on earth had worn enchanted flesh.

This sonnet is divided into three parts. In the first part I call upon and implore Love's faithful to weep, and I say that their lord himself weeps and that they, hearing the reason for his weeping, should be more disposed to hear me. In the second part I relate the cause. In the third part I speak of

an honour that Love bestowed upon this lady. The second
part begins: 'Love hears'; the third: 'Hear then how'.

> Brute death,* the enemy of tenderness,
>   timeless mother of grief,
>   judgement incontestable, severe—
>   for your sick source of grief within my heart,
>   that I must bear in misery,
>   my tongue consumes itself with cursing you.
>   And if I want to make you beg for mercy,
>   I only need reveal
>   your felonies, your guilt of every guilt;
>   not that you are not known for what you are,
>   but rather to inflame
>   whoever hopes for sustenance in love.
> You have bereft the world of gentlest grace,
>   of all that in sweet ladies merits praise;
>   in youth's gay tender years
>   you have destroyed all love's light-heartedness.
>   Who might this lady be I shall not say,
>   save that her qualities reveal her name;
>   who does not earn salvation,
>   let him not hope to share her company.

This sonnet is divided into four parts. In the first part
I address Death by certain appropriate names; in the second I tell why I curse it; in the third I revile it; in the
fourth I turn to speaking to an apparently indefinite person,
yet very definite to my mind. The second part begins: 'for
your sick source'; the third: 'And if I want'; the fourth: 'who
does not'.

IX

SOMETIME after the death of this lady it became necessary
for me to leave the previously mentioned city and go toward,
but not as far as, those parts where the lady who had
formerly acted as my screen was now staying. Truly enough,
I appeared to be in the company of others, but the journey
so irked me because I was going further away from my bliss,
that my sighs could hardly relieve the anguish of my heart.
Therefore his most sweet lordship, who ruled over me
through the power of the very gracious lady, took the shape
in my mind of a pilgrim* lightly and poorly clad. He seemed
to be disheartened; he stared at the ground except for the
times when his eyes seemed to turn toward a beautiful
stream,* swift and very clear, which flowed alongside the
path I was travelling. It seemed that Love called me and
spoke these words: 'I come from that lady who has been
your shield for so long a time; I know that she will not
return soon to your city, and so that heart which I made
you leave with her I now have with me and I am taking it
to a lady who will be your new defence as was the previous
one.' He named her, and I knew her well. 'If you should,
however, repeat any of the things I have told you, do so in
a way that will not disclose the pretended love which you
have shown for this lady, and which you will have to show
for another.' As he said these words, his image faded in my
mind, and suddenly Love became so great a part of me that,
as if transformed in my appearance, I rode on that day very
pensive and accompanied by many sighs. The next day I
began writing a sonnet which begins: 'As I rode out'.

> As I rode out one day not long ago
>   by narrow roads, and heavy with the thought
>   of what compelled my going, I met Love
>   in pilgrim's rags coming the other way.

All his appearance seemed to speak such grief
as kings might feel upon the loss of crown;
and ever sighing, bent with thought, he came,
his eyes averted from all passers-by.
Yet as we met he called to me by name
and said to me, 'I come from that far land,
where I had sent your heart to serve my will;
I bring it back* to court a new delight.'
And then so much of him was fused with me,
he vanished from my sight, I know not how.

This sonnet has three parts. In the first part I tell how I encountered Love and how he looked; in the second I relate what he told me, only partially, however, for fear of disclosing my secret; in the third part I tell how he vanished. The second part begins: 'Yet as we met'; the third: 'And then so much'.

X

AFTER returning from my journey I began looking for this lady that my lord had named while travelling the road of sighs. To make a long story short, in a brief time I made her so completely my defence that many people commented more than courtesy would permit; and so, I often found myself gravely concerned. For this reason, namely, the scandalous rumours that viciously stripped me of my good name, the most gracious Beatrice, scourge of vice and queen of virtue, passing along a certain street, denied me her most sweet greeting in which lay all my bliss. Now I find it necessary to depart from my subject for a while in order to make clear the powerful effect her greeting used to have on me.

XI

WHENEVER and wherever she appeared, in anticipation of her marvellous greeting, I held no man my enemy, and there burned within me a flame that consumed all past offences; and during this time if anyone had asked me about anything, my answer, with face free of all pride, could only have been 'Love'. And when she was about to greet me, one of Love's spirits, annihilating all the spirits of the senses, would drive out the feeble spirits of sight,* saying to them, 'Go and pay homage to your mistress'; and he would take their place. And whoever might have wished to know what Love is, could have done so by looking at my trembling eyes. And when this most gracious one's salutation greeted me, Love was no medium capable of my unbearable bliss, but rather, as if possessed with an excess of sweetness, he became such that my body, which was completely under his rule, often moved like a heavy inanimate object. Now it is most evident that in her salutation lay my blessed happiness, which many times exceeded and overflowed my brim.

XII

NOW, returning to my subject, after my blessed joy was denied me, I was so grief-stricken that withdrawing from all company, I went to a solitary place and bathed the earth with bitter tears. After my sobbing had subsided somewhat, I closed myself in my room where I could lament without being heard; and here, asking pity of the lady of courtesy* and calling, 'Love, help your faithful one', I fell asleep like a little boy crying from a spanking. While in the middle of my sleep, I seemed to see a young man in my room sitting near me dressed in the whitest clothes and apparently deeply concerned; he was looking at me where I lay, and having stared at me for some time, it seemed that, sighing, he called me and said these words: 'My son, it is time to do away with our pretences.'* Then I seemed to know who he was, because many times before, in my sleep, he had called to me in the same way; and as I looked at him, it seemed to me that he was weeping with compassion and that he seemed anxious that I speak to him. Encouraged by this, I began to address him, saying: 'Lord of all virtues, why do you weep?' And he said to me: 'I am like the centre of a circle, equidistant from all points on the circumference, but you are not.'*

Then I pondered his words and they were obscure to me, and so I gathered my courage and said: 'What is this, my Lord, that you speak so obscurely?' And this time he spoke in Italian, saying: 'Do not ask more than is useful to you.' So then I began talking instead about the greeting that had been denied me; and when I asked him why, he answered: 'Our Beatrice heard from the talk of certain people that the lady I named to you on the road of sighs was being harmed by you. Therefore, this most gracious one, who is contrary to all harm, deigned not to greet you, fearing your person to be a source of harm to her. Since your long-kept secret is in truth partially known to her, I want you to write a poem in which you mention the power I have over you through her, and the fact that ever since you were a boy you have belonged to her; and on this point, call in witness him who knows, and beg him to testify to her. And I, who am that witness, will gladly explain it to her, and from this she will understand your true feeling; and understanding it, she will also set the proper value on the words of those people who were mistaken about you. Let these words be as it were an intermediary so that you do not speak directly to her, for it is not fitting that you should; and except in my company, do not send these words to any place where she could hear them; be sure, however, to enhance them with sweet music in which I shall be present whenever the necessity occurs.' Having said this, he disappeared, and my sleep was broken. Whereupon I, thinking back, discovered that the vision had appeared to me during the ninth hour of the day; and before I left my room I resolved to write a ballad* in which I would follow the instructions my lord had given me. And later on I composed this ballad which begins: 'Ballad I wish'.

> Ballad, I wish for you to seek out Love
>   and go with him into my lady's presence,
>   so that my exculpation, which you sing,
>   may be explained to her by Love, my lord.
> You travel, ballad, with such graciousness
>   that even without companions
> you well could venture boldly anywhere;
> but if with full assurance you would go,
> first go in search of Love;
> perhaps to go without him is unwise,
> because that one who is to hear you speak
> is angry with me now, or so I think.
> So, were you not accompanied by him,
> most easily she might receive you ill.
> With sweetness singing, in Love's company,
>   begin to sound these words
>   after your first entreaty for compassion:
> 'My lady, he who sends me to you, wishes

that, if it's to your liking
you hear me out and judge if he's excused.
With me is Love, who through your beauty's power
at will can make his whole appearance change:
judge for yourself why Love made his eyes rove,
remembering his heart has never strayed.'
Tell her: 'My lady, his heart has remained
so solid in its faith
that every thought makes him a slave to you;
first was he yours and never has he strayed.'
If she should not believe you,
tell her to question Love, who knows the truth.
Ask her with humble prayer before you end,
if pardon be too troublesome to give,
that she send orders to me that I die,
and faithfully her servant will obey.
And tell Love, who is all compassion's key,
before you take your leave,
and who knows how to tell her my excuse:
'In recompense of my sweet melody
remain awhile with her,
talk to her of your servant as you will;
and if your prayer should win for him reprieve,
let peace be promised him by her clear smile.'
My gracious ballad, if it please you, go,
win yourself honour when the time is ripe.

This ballad is divided into three parts. In the first I tell
it where to go and encourage it so that it will go with more
assurance, and I tell it whose company it is to seek if it
wishes to go securely and free from any danger; in the
second I tell it what it is supposed to make known; in the
third I allow it to depart whenever it pleases, commending
its going to the arms of fortune. The second part begins
here: 'With sweetness singing'; the third here: 'My gracious
ballad'.

One might oppose me and say that he did not know to
whom my words in the second person were addressed, since
the ballad is nothing more than the words I myself speak;
and therefore, I say that I intend to solve and clear up this

uncertainty in an even more difficult section of this little book, and then he who may be in doubt here or who may wish to object in the above fashion, let him understand* the explanation to apply here as well.

XIII

AFTER this last vision, when I had already written the words Love had imposed on me to write, many and diversified thoughts, against which I was defenceless, began to assail and try me. Among these thoughts were four that seemed to hinder most my peace of mind. The first was this: the lordship of Love is good since he diverts the mind of his faithful from all evil things. The next was this: the lordship of Love is evil, because the more fidelity his faithful one bears him, the more grave and pitiful are the tribulations he must endure. Another was this: the name of Love is so sweet to hear that it seems impossible to me that the effect itself could be in most things other than sweet, since names follow from the things they name, as the saying goes: 'Names are the consequences of things.'* The fourth was this: the lady through whom Love binds you so is not like other ladies, that her heart can be easily moved. And each one of these thoughts assailed me so that I felt like one who does not know what direction to take, who wants to start but does not know which way to go. And as for trying to find a common road for all of them, that is, a place where all should come together, this was a way very alien to me; namely, calling upon Pity and throwing myself into her arms. While I was in this condition, the desire to write some poetry came to me, so I wrote this sonnet which begins: 'All my thoughts'.

All my thoughts are telling me of Love;
    they have in them such great diversity
    that one thought makes me welcome all his power,
    another thinks Love's power is insane,
    another makes me hope and brings delight,
    another moves me oftentimes to tears.
    Only in begging pity all agree,

and tremble as they do with fearful heart.
Now I know not from which to take my cue;
  I want to speak but know not what to say.
  Thus do I wander in a maze of Love!
  And if I want to harmonize these thoughts,
  to do so I must call upon my foe,
  by asking Lady Pity for defence.

This sonnet can be divided into four parts. In the first I say and submit that all my thoughts are of Love; in the second I say that they are different, and I mention their differences; in the third I tell in what way they all seem to be in accord; in the fourth I say that, wishing to speak of Love, I know not where to take my cue, and if I wish to take it from all of them, it becomes necessary for me to call upon my foe, my Lady Pity. I say 'Lady' in an almost scornful manner of speaking. The second part begins here: 'they have in them'; the third here: 'Only in begging'; the fourth here: 'Now I know not'.

XIV

AFTER the battle* of the conflicting thoughts, it happened that my most gracious lady went to a place where many worthy ladies were gathered. I was taken to this place by a friend who believed he was giving me great delight by taking me to such a place where many ladies displayed their beauty. Then I, scarcely knowing for what purpose I was brought there and trusting in the friend who had led me to the very threshold of death, said to him: 'Why have we come to these ladies?' He answered me: 'So that they may be worthily attended.' The truth is that they were gathered here in the company of a respected lady who had been married that day; and so, according to the custom of the aforementioned city,* they were supposed to keep her company during her first meal at the home of her bridegroom. So I, thinking to please my friend in so doing, decided to remain with him in attendance upon the ladies. No sooner had I reached my decision than I seemed to feel a strange throbbing in the left side of my chest which before long spread to all parts of my body. Then, so as not to attract attention, I leaned against a painting that ran along the walls of that house, and fearing that people might have become aware of my trembling, I raised my eyes and, gazing at the ladies, I saw among them the most gracious Beatrice. Then my spirits were so disrupted* by the strength that Love acquired when he saw himself so close to the most gracious lady, that none remained alive except the spirits of sight; and even these remained outside their instruments, because Love usurped their enviable seat to view the marvellous lady. And even though I was not myself, I was still very moved by these little spirits that bitterly protested, saying: 'If this one had not knocked us from our position like a bolt of lightning, we too could have stayed to see the wonders of this lady as all our peers are doing.' I know that many of these ladies, becoming aware of my transfiguration, began to marvel, and speaking with that most gracious one, they mocked me. Then my friend, who in good faith had been deceived, took me by the hand and leading me out of the sight of these ladies, asked me what was the matter. And I, somewhat restored, feeling my dead spirits come back to life and the ejected ones return to their possessions, said these words to my friend: 'I have placed my feet on those boundaries of life beyond which no one can go further and hope to return.'* Leaving him, I returned to my room of tears, in which, weeping and ashamed, I said to myself: 'If this lady were aware of my condition, I do not believe she would mock my appearance as she did, but rather I believe she would feel great pity.' And in the midst of my tears, I decided to write a few words addressed to her explaining the reason for my transfiguration and saying that I well know that people are not aware of it and that were they aware of it, they would be moved to pity. And I resolved to say these words with the hope that perchance they would reach her ears. Then I composed this sonnet which begins: 'You join with other ladies'.

You join with other ladies to deride me
   and do not think, my lady, for what cause
   I cut so awkward and grotesque a figure
   when I stand gazing at your lovely form.
   Could you but know my soul in charity,
   then yours would melt from its accustomed scorn;
   for Love, when he beholds me near to you,
   takes on a cruel and bold new confidence
and puts my frightened senses to the sword,
   murdering this one, driving that one out,
   till only he is left to look at you;
   thus, though his changeling, I am not so changed
   but that I still can hear in my own soul
   my outcast senses mourning in their pain.

Since the division is made only to help reveal the meaning of the thing divided, I do not divide this sonnet, and since what has been said of its occasion is sufficiently clear, there is no need for division. True, among the words in which I relate the occasion for this sonnet there occur certain confusing expressions, as when I say that Love slays all my spirits and only those of vision remain, and they outside their instruments. This uncertainty is impossible to resolve for one who is not in like degree a faithful follower of Love; to one who is, that which would resolve the uncertainty is already clear. And so, it is not wise for me to clear up such uncertainties, for my words of clarification would be meaningless to some and superfluous to others.

XV

AFTER this strange transfiguration an intense thought came
to me, one which seldom left me but rather continually
oppressed me and spoke to me in this way: 'Since you take
on so ridiculous an appearance whenever you are near this
lady, why do you try to see her? Assume that she were to
ask you this, and that all your faculties were free to answer
her, what would your answer be?' And to this another
humble thought replied, saying: 'If I did not lose my powers
and were free enough to be able to answer her, I would tell
her that no sooner do I call to mind the astonishing image
of her beauty than the desire to see her overtakes me, and
this desire is so powerful that it slays and destroys in my
memory anything that might rise to restrain it; therefore,
past sufferings do not hold me back from trying to behold
her.' Moved by such thoughts, I decided to write a few
words in which, exonerating myself from blame on this
occasion, I would also include what happens to me whenever
I am near her. Then I wrote this sonnet which begins: 'What
could restrain me'.

> What could restrain me dies out of my mind
>   when I stand in your presence, my heart's bliss;
>   when I am near you Love is there to warn:
>   'Run, run the other way if you fear death.'
>   My blanching face reveals my fainting heart,
>   which growing fainter looks for some support,
>   and as I tremble in this drunken state
>   it seems that every stone is shouting 'Die!'
> He sins who witnesses my desperate state
>   and does not try to comfort my torn heart,
>   though it were but the slightest show of grief,
>   for pity's sake, that by your mocking dies,
>   once brought to life within my dying face,
>   whose yearning eyes call death to take me now.

This sonnet is divided into two parts. In the first I give the reason why I do not stop myself from seeking this lady's company; in the second I tell what happens to me when I go near her, and I begin this part: 'When I am near you'. This second part in turn divides again into five, according to five different subjects. In the first I relate that which Love, counselled by reason, tells me whenever I am near her; in the second I express the condition of my heart through the example of my face; in the third I tell how all assurance grows faint in me; in the fourth I stress that he sins who does not show pity, the sign of which would be of some comfort to me; in the last part I tell why one should have pity, namely, because of the piteous look which fills my eyes, a piteous look which is destroyed and never seen by anyone, all because of the mocking of this lady who causes others, who perhaps might have seen this pity, to do as she does. The second part begins here: 'My blanching face'; the third: 'and as I tremble'; the fourth: 'He sins'; the fifth: 'for pity's sake'.

XVI

AFTER completing this last sonnet I was moved by a desire to write more poetry in which I should mention four more things that, it seemed to me, had not yet been made clear. The first of these is that many times I grieved when my memory excited my imagination to think of the transformations that Love worked in me. The second is that Love, many times without warning, attacked me so violently that no part of me remained alive except one thought that spoke of this lady. The third is that when this battle of Love raged within me so, I went in all my pallor to behold this lady, believing that the sight of her would defend me in this battle,* but forgetting what happens to me whenever I approach such abundant graciousness. The fourth is that not only did this sight not defend me but it ultimately annihilated my little remaining life. Therefore I composed this sonnet, which begins: 'So many times'.

> So many times there comes into my mind
>   the dark condition Love bestows on me,
> that pity comes and often makes me say:
> 'Could anyone have ever felt the same?'
> So forcefully and suddenly Love strikes
> that my life would all but abandon me
> were it not for one last surviving spirit,
> allowed to live because it speaks of you.
> Hoping to help myself, I gather courage
>   and pale and drawn and lacking all defence,
> I come to see you hoping to be healed;
> but if I raise my eyes to look at you
> a trembling starts at once within my heart
> and drives life out and stops my pulses' beat.

This sonnet is divided into four parts according to the four things it speaks of, and since they are explained above,

I concern myself only with indicating the parts by their beginnings; the second part begins here: 'So forcefully'; the third here: 'Hoping to help myself'; the fourth here: 'but if I raise'.

XVII

AFTER I had written these three sonnets in which I spoke to this lady, and in which little concerning my condition was left untold, believing I should be silent and say no more about this, since it seemed to me that I had sufficiently indicated my condition to her and because I should never again address my poems to her, it became essential for me to take up a new theme, one more lofty than the last. Since I think the occasion for my new theme offers pleasant listening, I shall tell about it as briefly as possible.

XVIII

BECAUSE through my appearance many people had learned of the secret of my heart, certain ladies, gathered together and enjoying each other's company, knew my heart well, for each of them had seen me swoon at one time or another. As if guided by fortune, one day I was passing near them when one of these worthy ladies called to me. The lady who addressed me had a very pleasing manner of speaking, and when I stood before this group of ladies and saw that my most gracious lady was not among them, gaining confidence, I greeted them and asked what I could do to please them. There were many ladies present, some of whom were laughing among themselves. There were others who looked at me anxiously, waiting for me to say something. There were others who spoke among themselves, one of whom, directing her eyes toward me and calling my name, said to me: 'To what end do you love this lady if you cannot even endure the sight of her? Tell us, for surely the purpose of such love must be strange indeed.' After she had said these words, not only she but all the others began with expectant faces to await my answer. Then I said to them: 'Ladies, the end and aim of my love formerly lay in the greeting of this lady to whom you are perhaps referring, and in this greeting dwelt my bliss which was the end of all my desires. But since it pleased her to deny it to me, my lord, Love, through his grace, has placed all my bliss in something that cannot fail me.' Then these ladies began speaking among themselves, and just as sometimes the rain can be seen falling mingled with beautiful flakes of snow, so did I seem to hear their words coming forth mingled with sighs. And after these ladies had spoken among themselves awhile, the lady who had first addressed me spoke to me again, saying: 'We beg you to tell us wherein this bliss of yours now lies.' And I answered her by saying: 'In those words that praise my lady.' Then she who had asked the question responded: 'If you are telling us the truth, then those words you wrote to her indicating your condition must have been composed with other intentions.' Then I, thinking of these words that shamed me, departed from these ladies saying to myself: 'Since there is so much bliss in those words that praise my lady, why have I ever spoken otherwise?' Therefore, I resolved that from then on I would choose material for my poems that should be in praise of this most gracious one. After reflecting much on such a decision, it seemed to me that I had undertaken too lofty a theme for myself, so that I dared not begin writing, and I remained for several days afterwards with the desire to write and the fear of beginning.

XIX

THEN it happened that while walking down a road along
which ran a very clear stream, I was so seized by the desire
to compose poetry that I began thinking of how I should
go about it. I thought that to speak of my lady would not
be becoming unless I were to speak to ladies in the second
person, and not to just any ladies, but only to those who
are worthy and not merely women. Then my tongue, moving almost of its own accord, spoke and said: 'Ladies
refined and sensitive in Love'. With great delight I stored
these words away in my memory, thinking to use them as
an opening to my poem. Then after returning to the aforementioned city and musing for several days, I began to write
a *canzone** using this beginning and arranged it in a way
that will be seen below in its division. The *canzone* begins:
'Ladies, refined and sensitive'.

> Ladies, refined and sensitive in Love,
> > I wish to speak with you about my lady,
> > not thinking to complete her litany,
> > but talking, which perhaps may ease my mind.
> > When I reflect upon her worthiness
> > a love so sweet makes itself felt in me
> > that if at that point courage did not fail
> > my discourse would make lovers of you all.
> > I do not wish to choose a lofty tone,
> > for fear that my song fail and turn me base;
> > but I shall tell you of her gracious state,
> > defectively, to measure by her merit,
> > ladies and maidens sensitive in Love,
> > for such a thing is not for others' ears.
> The mind of God receives an angel's prayer
> > that says: 'My Lord, on earth is seen
> > a living miracle proceeding from
> a soul whose light reaches as far as here.'

Heaven, that lacks its full perfection only
in lacking her, asks for her of its Lord,
and every saint is begging for this favour.
Compassion for his creatures still remains,
for God replies, referring to my lady:
'My chosen ones, now suffer peacefully,
and while it pleases me, let your hope stay
with one down there who dreads the loss of her,
who when in hell shall say unto the damned,*
"I have beheld the hope of heaven's blessed." '
My lady is desired in highest heaven;
I want to tell you what her power does:
a lady who aspires to graciousness
should seek her company, for when she walks,
Love drives a killing frost into vile hearts
that freezes and destroys their every thought;
and dare a thought remain to look at her
it has to change to good or else must die;
and if she finds one worthy to behold her,
he feels her power, for her least salutation
bestows salvation on this favoured one
and humbles him till he forgets all wrongs.
This too has God Almighty graced her with:
whoever speaks with her shall speak with Him.
Love says of her: 'How can flesh drawn from clay,
achieve such beauty and such purity?'
He looks again and to himself he swears
that God intended something new for earth.
Her colour is the paleness of the pearl,
in measure suited* to her graciousness;
she is the highest nature can achieve
and by her mould all beauty tests itself.
From out her eyes, wherever they may move
come spirits that are all aflame with Love;
they pierce the eyes of any one that looks
and pass straight through till each one finds the heart;
upon her face you see depicted Love,
there where none dares to hold his gaze too long.
My song, I know that you will go and speak
to many ladies when I bid you leave.

And now I warn you, since I raised you, song,
as Love's true child, ingenuous and plain,
whomever you should meet, with kindness pray:
'Please help me find my way, for I am meant
to reach that one whose praises are my dress.'
And, that your going will not be in vain,
do not waste time with any vulgar folk;
endeavour, if you can, to show yourself
only to men and ladies who are worthy;
they will direct you by the quickest path
and lead you to this lady and to Love.
Speak well of me to Love as well you should.

In order that this *canzone* may be better understood, I shall divide it more carefully than the previous poems. First I divide it into three parts. The first part is a preface to the words that follow; the second is the intended subject; the third is a sort of handmaiden to the words which precede it. The second part begins: 'The mind'; the third: 'My song, I know that you'. Now the first part subdivides into four. In the first I declare to whom I wish to speak about my lady and why I wish to speak; in the second I tell in what condition I seem to find myself whenever I think of her worthiness and what I would say if I did not lose courage; in the third I tell how I intend to speak of her in order not to be hindered by baseness; in the fourth, mentioning once again to whom I intend to speak, I give the reason why it is to them I speak. The second subdivision begins here: 'When I reflect'; the third here: 'I do not wish'; the fourth: 'ladies and maidens'. When I say, 'The mind', then I begin to deal with this lady, and this part is subdivided into two. In the first I tell how she is thought of in heaven; in the second I tell how she is thought of on earth, beginning here: 'My lady is desired'. This second part divides further into two. In the first part I speak of her in respect to the magnificence of her soul, relating examples of the wondrous powers that proceed from her soul; in the second I speak of her in respect to the magnificence of her visible qualities, mentioning some of her beauties with the words, 'Love says of her'. This second part is further divided into two. In the first I speak of certain beauties pertaining to her whole body; in the second I speak of certain beauties pertaining to particular parts of her body, beginning: 'From out her eyes'. This is again divided in two. First I speak of her eyes, which are the initiators of love; next I speak of her mouth,* which is the supreme desire of my love. So that here and now every perverse thought may be extinguished, let him who reads this remember what has been mentioned previously concerning this lady's greeting, which is an act performed by her mouth; namely, that it was the goal of all my desire so long as I was able to receive it. Then when I say, 'My song, I know that you', I am adding a stanza as a handmaiden* to the others. In this stanza I tell what I desire of my song, and because this last part is easy to understand, I do not bother to divide it further. Certainly, to make the meaning more apparent, I would have to make my divisions more extensive; nevertheless, if there are people who do not have wit enough to understand* the poem by the divisions already made, it would not displease me if they would leave it alone; for certainly I fear I have communicated its meaning to too many through the divisions I have already made, if it come about that many read them.

XX

AS a result of this *canzone* becoming somewhat known to people, one of my friends happened to hear it, and was moved to ask me* for my definition of Love, having acquired from my words, perhaps, confidence in me beyond my worth. Therefore, thinking that after such words it would be good to say something about the nature of Love, and thinking to oblige my friend, I decided to compose a poem dealing with Love. Then I wrote this sonnet, which begins: 'Love and the gracious heart'.

> Love and the gracious heart are but one thing,
>   as that wise poet* puts it in his poem;
>   as much can one without the other be
>   as without reason can the reasoning mind.
>   Nature creates them when in loving mood,
>   Love to be king, the heart to be his home,
>   a place where Love inactive lies in wait
>   sometimes a longer, now a shorter time.
> A worthy lady's beauty next is viewed
>   with pleasure by the eyes, and in the heart
>   desire for the pleasing thing is born,
>   and for awhile this beauty lingers there
>   until Love's spirit is aroused from sleep.
>   A man of worth with ladies does the same.

This sonnet divides into two parts. In the first I speak of Love as a potential force;* in the second I speak of it as a power brought into action. The second begins here: 'A worthy lady's beauty'. The first part divides again in two. First, I tell in what thing this power exists; second, I tell how this thing and this power are together brought into being and how one is related to the other just as form is to matter.* The second begins here: 'Nature creates them'. Then when I say, 'A worthy lady's beauty', I explain how this power is brought into action: first how it works in men, then how it works with ladies, beginning here: 'A man of worth'.

XXI

AFTER having dealt with Love in the last sonnet, I had a desire to write more, this time in praise of that most gracious lady, using words to show how it is through her that Love is awakened and how she not only awakens him there where he sleeps, but also how she, miraculously working, brings him into existence there where he is not. Then I wrote this sonnet which begins: 'The power of Love'.

> The power of Love borne in my lady's eyes
>   imparts its grace to all she looks upon;
> men turn to gaze at her when she walks by;
> the heart of him she greets is made to quake,
> his face to whiten, forcing down his gaze;
> he sighs as all his defects flash in mind;
> all pride and indignation flee from her.
> Help me to honour her, most gracious ladies.
> All sweet conception, every humblest thought
>   blooms in the heart of one who hears her speak,
>   and man is blessed at his first sight of her.
> The image of her when she starts to smile
> breaks out of words, the mind cannot contain it,
> a miracle too rich and strange to hold.

This sonnet has three parts. In the first I tell how this lady animates this power by the use of her most munificent eyes; in the third I tell how she does the same thing, only this time by the use of her most gracious mouth; and between these two is a very small part, which is like a beggar asking aid from the preceding and following parts, and it begins here: 'Help me to honour her'. The third begins here: 'All sweet conception'. The first part divides further into three. In the first I tell how she miraculously makes gracious whatever she looks upon, and this is as much as to say that she brings Love into potential existence there where he does not exist; in the second part I tell how she animates Love in the hearts of those who behold her; in the third I tell of what she then effects in their hearts. The second part begins here: 'men turn to gaze'; and the third here: 'the heart of him she greets'. Then when I say, 'Help me to honour', I indicate to whom I am speaking by calling upon ladies for their assistance in honouring my lady. Then when I say, 'All sweet conception', I repeat what I said in the first part, using, this time, two actions of her mouth: the first is her sweet manner of speaking, the second is her miraculous smile. I do not mention how this last act of her mouth works in the hearts of people because the memory is not capable of retaining the image of such a smile nor of its effects.

XXII

NOT many days after this, according to the will of the Lord of Glory (who did not refuse death for Himself) he who had been the father* of such great splendour as this most gracious Beatrice was, departing from this life, passed most certainly into eternal glory. Since such a departure is sorrowful to those who remain and who have been friends of the deceased; and since there is no friendship more intimate than that of a good father for a good child or of a good child for a good father; and since this lady possessed the highest degree of goodness; and since her father, as is believed by many and it is the truth, was exceedingly good—then it is clear that this lady was bitterly filled with sorrow.

And inasmuch as, according to the customs of this city, ladies should gather with ladies and men with men on such occasions, many ladies were assembled in that place where Beatrice wept pathetically. I saw several of them returning from her house and heard their words concerning this most gracious one and how she grieved. Among these words I heard: 'Truly, she grieves so, that whoever were to see her would die of pity.' Then these ladies passed by me, and I was left so full of sorrow that tears kept running down my face, forcing me to cover my eyes with my hands. And had it not been that I expected to hear more about her, since I was situated at a point where most of those ladies taking leave of her would pass me by, I would have hidden myself as soon as the tears had overcome me. And while I remained longer in the same place, other ladies passed by me talking to each other as they went, saying: 'Who among us could ever again be happy after hearing this lady speak so piteously?' After these, other ladies passed and as they passed said: 'This man here is weeping as though he had seen her as we have.' Then others said of me: 'Look at this man; he does not seem to be himself, so changed he is!' And so with this passage of ladies, I heard words spoken of her and me in the manner just described. After thinking about it for a while, I decided to write (since I had a worthy reason to express myself in poetry) and to include in my words all that I had heard from these ladies. And since I would willingly have questioned them had I not thought it indiscreet, I treated my theme as if I had asked them questions and they had answered me.* And I composed two sonnets. In the first I ask those questions which I had wanted to ask; in the other I give their answer, taking that which I heard them speak and using it as if they had said it in reply to me. The first begins: 'O you who come'; the other: 'Are you the one'.

> O you who come this way so mournfully,
>   with downcast eyes in witness of your pain,
>   where were you that the colour of your cheeks
>   appears to have become like that of grief?
>   Is it our sweetest lady you have seen
>   bathing with tears Love's image in her face?
>   O ladies, tell me, for my heart tells me:
>   it is her grace that graces so your mien.
> And if you come from so profound a grief,
>   may it please you to stay with me a while
>   and tell me truly what you know of her.
>   I see your eyes, I see how they have wept,
>   and how you come retreating all undone;
>   my heart is touched and shaken at the sight.

This sonnet divides into two parts. In the first I call upon these ladies and ask them if they come from my lady, telling them that I believe that they do since they return as if made more gracious; in the second I ask them to talk to me about her. The second part begins: 'And if you come'.

Following is the other sonnet, as explained previously:

> Are you the one that often spoke to us
>   about our lady, and to us alone?
>   You do in sound of voice resemble him,
>   but in your face we find another's look.

What causes you to shed such bitter tears,
that makes us melt with pity at their sight?
Perhaps you saw her weeping and cannot
conceal the sorrow in your aching heart?
To us leave grieving and the tearful way
(to comfort us would be a grave offence)
for we have heard her speak amid her sobs.
Her face proclaims the agony she feels;
if one of us had wished to look at it,
that one had died of sorrow then and there.

This sonnet has four parts according to the four responses
of the ladies through whom I speak, and since they are
evident enough in the sonnet, I do not bother explaining
the meaning of the parts but merely indicate where they
occur. The second begins: 'What causes you'; the third: 'To
us leave grieving'; the fourth: 'Her face proclaims'.

XXIII

A FEW days after this, it happened that a severe illness overtook part of my body and caused me to suffer intense pain constantly for nine days, which in turn made me so weak that it became necessary for me to lie in bed like a paralysed person. On the ninth day, experiencing unbearable pain, I had a thought concerning my lady. After thinking about her a while, I returned to thoughts of my frail life, and realizing how short life is, even if one is healthy, I began to sob inwardly at such misery. Then sighing loudly, I said to myself: 'Some day the most gracious Beatrice will surely have to die.' I went so out of my head that I closed my eyes and became convulsed as one in a delirium and began to have these imaginings: how at the outset of my imagination's wandering certain faces of ladies with dishevelled hair appeared to me and they were saying: 'You too shall die.' And then after these ladies there appeared to me certain faces, strange and horrible to behold, saying to me: 'You are dead.' As my imagination wandered in this fashion, I came to such a point that I no longer knew where I was. I seemed to see ladies amazingly sad, weeping as they made their way down a street, their hair dishevelled; I seemed to see the sun darken in a way that gave the stars a colour that would have made me swear that they were weeping; it seemed to me that the birds flying through the air fell to earth dead, and that there were great earthquakes.*

Astonished and very frightened, I imagined that a certain friend came to me and said: 'You do not know then that your miraculous lady has departed from this life?' At that I began to sob most piteously, not only in my dream, but with my eyes that were wet with real tears. I imagined I was looking up at the sky, and I seemed to see a multitude of angels, and in front of them was a little pure-white cloud. It seemed to me that these angels were singing in glory, and the words of their song seemed to be these: 'Hosanna in the highest',* and the rest I could not hear. Then it seemed that my heart, in which so much love dwelt, said to me: 'True it is that our lady lies dead.' And so it seemed to me that I went to see the body in which that most worthy and blessed soul had dwelt, and so strong was the hallucination that it actually showed me this lady dead. And it seemed that ladies were covering her head with a white veil, and it seemed that her face was so filled with joyous acceptance that it said to me: 'I am contemplating the fountainhead of peace.' Through seeing her in this dream I became filled with such humility that I called upon Death and said: 'Sweet death, come to me and do not be unkind, for you have just been in a place that must have made you gracious. Come to me now, for I earnestly desire you; you can see that I do, for already I wear your colour.' And when I had seen that the rites usually performed on the body of the dead had been administered, it seemed that I returned to my room and from there looked toward heaven; and so vivid was my dream that, weeping, I began to cry aloud in my real voice: 'O most beautiful soul, how blessed is he who beholds you!'

As I was saying these words in a spasm of tears and calling upon death to come to me, a young and gracious lady,* who had been at my bedside, believing that my sobbing and my words had been due only to the pain of my illness, began in great fright to weep. Then other ladies who were about the room became aware of my weeping through seeing this one weeping, and after making this one, who was a close relative of mine, leave me, believing that I was dreaming, drew close to waken me, saying: 'Wake up,' and 'Don't be afraid.' As they spoke in this fashion, my realistic dream was broken at the moment when I was about to say, 'Oh, Beatrice, blessed you are.' And I had already said, 'Oh, Beatrice,' when I opened my eyes with a start and saw that I was deceived. Although I had uttered this name, my voice had been so broken by my sobs and tears that I think these ladies were not able to understand. Even though I was very much ashamed, I nevertheless turned toward them, thanks to some warning from Love. And when they saw me, they began saying, 'He looks as if he were dead,' and to each other, 'Let us try to comfort him'; and so they said many things to comfort me and then asked me what had frightened me so. Having been comforted somewhat and having recognized the falseness of my imagining, I answered them: 'I shall tell you what happened to me.' Then I began from the beginning and continued to the very end, telling them what I had seen but keeping silent the name of the most gracious one. After I was cured of my illness, I decided to write about what had happened to me, because I thought it would be a fascinating thing to hear about. And so I composed this *canzone*:* 'A very young and sympathetic lady' which is constructed in the manner made clear in the divisions following it.

A very young and sympathetic lady,
 extremely graced with human gentleness,
 who stood by me and heard me call on death,
 seeing the piteous weeping of my eyes
 and hearing wild, confusing words I spoke,
 became so filled with fear she wept aloud.
 Then other ladies, made aware of me
 through that one weeping there beside my bed,
 forced her to go away
 and then drew near to bring me to my senses.
 One said to me: 'Wake up,'
 another said: 'Why are you so distressed?'
With this I left the world of my strange dream,
calling aloud the name of my dear lady.
I called with voice so weak and filled with pain
 and broken so by tears and anguished sobs,
 that my heart only heard her name called out.
 Although there was a look of deep-felt shame
 that made itself stand out upon my face,
 Love made me look these ladies in the eye.
 The pallor of my face amazed them so,
 they could not help but start to speak of death.
 'Oh, let us comfort him,'
 implored one lady sweetly of another.

And many times they said:
'What did you see that took away your strength?'
Consoled and comforted somewhat, I said:
'Ladies, now I shall tell you what I saw.'
While I was brooding on my languid life,
    and sensed how fleeting is our little day,
    Love wept within my heart which is his home;
    and then my startled soul went numb with fear,
    and sighing deep within myself, I said:
    'My lady some day surely has to die.'
    Then taken by this fright and wonderment,
    I closed my heavy wept-out tired eyes,
    and so despaired and weak
    were all my spirits, that each went drifting off;
    and then drifting and dreaming
    with consciousness and truth left far behind,
    I saw the looks of ladies wild with wrath
    who kept on telling me, 'You'll die, you'll die.'
Then, drifting in my false imaginings
    and standing in a place unknown to me,
    I seemed to be aware of dreadful things:
    of ladies all dishevelled as they walked,
    some weeping, others voicing their laments
    that with grief's flame-tipped arrows pierced my heart.
    and then it seemed to me I saw the sun
    grow slowly darker and a star appear,
    And sun and star were weeping;
    the birds flying above fell dead to earth;
        the earth began to quake.
        And then a man appeared, pale-faced and hoarse
        And said to me: 'Have you not heard the news?
        Your lady, once so lovely, now lies dead.'
    I raised my tear-bathed eyes to look above
        and saw, what seemed to be a rain of manna,
        the angels that ascended to the heavens;
        in front of them they had a little cloud;
        they sang; 'Hosanna' as they rose with it—
        I would have told you if they had said more.
        Then Love said: 'I'll not hide a thing from you;
        come now to see our lady lying dead.'

My false imaginings
led me to see my lady who was dead,
and as I looked at her
I saw that ladies hid her with a cloth.
Her face displayed such joyful resignation
it was as if she said: 'I am in peace.'
  So humbly in my grief I then beheld
what humble sweetness took its shape in her
that I said: 'Death, I hold you very dear;
by now you ought to be a gracious thing
and should have changed your scorn for sympathy,
since in my lady you have been at home.
I yearn so to become one of your own
that I resemble you in every way.
My heart begs you to come.'
When the last rites were done, I left that place,
and when I was alone
and looking toward high heaven, I exclaimed:
'Blessed is he who sees you, lovely soul!'
Just then you called me and thank God you did.

This *canzone* has two sections. In the first I tell, speaking
to some unidentified person, how I was aroused from a
delirious dream by certain ladies and how I promised to tell
them about it; in the second I relate how I told them. The
second begins here: 'While I was brooding'. The first section
divides into two parts. In the first I mention what certain
ladies and one particular lady said and did on account of
my dreaming before I had returned to true consciousness;
in the second I tell what these ladies said to me after I had
come out of my frenzied dream, and this part begins here:
'I called with voice'. Then when I say, 'While I was
brooding', I tell what I told them about my dream, and this
section has two parts. In the first I relate the dream
sequence; in the second I tell at what point I was called and
awakened, and with guarded words, I thank them for doing
so. And I begin this part here: 'Just then you called'.

XXIV

AFTER this unreal dream, one day I happened to be sitting in a certain place and meditating, when I felt a tremor begin in my heart, as if I were in the presence of my lady. Then a vision of Love came to me, and I seemed to see him coming from the place where my lady dwelt, and he seemed to speak joyfully from inside my heart: 'See that you bless the day that I took you captive, since it is your duty to do so.' And it seemed to me that my heart was happy, and because of its new condition, it did not seem that it could be my heart. Shortly after my heart said these words, using Love's tongue to speak, I saw coming toward me a worthy lady noted for her beauty who had been formerly the much-loved lady of my first friend.* And her name was Joan, but because of her beauty, as many believed, she had been given the name of Primavera, meaning Spring, and so she was called. And I looked behind her and saw the miraculous Beatrice coming. These ladies passed close by me, one behind the other, and it seemed that Love spoke in my heart and said: 'The one in front is called Primavera only because of the way in which she comes today; for I inspired the giver of her name to call her Primavera, meaning "she will come first" (*prima verrà*) on the day that Beatrice shows herself after the dream of her faithful one. And if you will also consider her real name, you will see that it too means *prima verrà*, since the name Joan comes from the name of that John (Giovanni) who preceded the True Light, saying: "I am the voice of one crying in the wilderness. Prepare ye the way of the Lord." '* After this, he seemed to speak again and say these words: 'Anyone of subtle discernment would call Beatrice Love, because she so greatly resembles me.' Then reflecting some more, I decided to write in verse to my first friend, whose heart, I believed, still held admiration for the radiant Primavera, not mentioning certain

things that should be kept silent. And I wrote this sonnet,
which begins: 'I felt a sleeping spirit'.

> I felt a sleeping spirit in my heart
>   awake to Love, and then from far away
>   I saw the Lord of Love approaching me,
>   and hardly recognized him through his joy.
>   'Think now of nothing but to honour me,'
>   I heard him say and each word was a smile;
>   and as my master stayed awhile with me,
>   I looked along the way that he had come
> and saw the Lady Joan and Lady Bice*
>   advancing toward the place in which I stood:
>   a miracle upon a miracle!
>   And as my memory tells me of it now,
>   Love said to me: 'The first of these is Spring,
>   and she who so resembles me is Love.'

This sonnet has many parts. The first of these tells how
I felt the accustomed tremor awaken in my heart and how
it seemed that Love revealed himself to me all joyous in my
heart coming from a faraway place; the second mentions
how it seemed Love spoke to me in my heart and how he
looked to me; the third tells how, after he had remained
awhile with me, I saw and heard certain things. The second
part begins: 'Think now of'; the third here: 'and as my
master'. The third part divides in two. In the first I mention
what I saw; in the second I tell what I heard. The second
begins here: 'Love said to me'.

XXV

IT may be that at this point some person, worthy of having every doubt cleared up, could be puzzled at my speaking of Love as if it were a thing in itself,* as if it were not only an intellectual substance but also a bodily substance. This in all truth is false, for Love does not exist in itself as a substance, but rather it is an accident in substance. And that I speak of Love as if he possessed a body, further still, as if he were a man, is evident from three things I say about him. I say that I saw him coming; and since 'to come' implies locomotion, and since, according to the Philosopher,* only a body may move through its own power from place to place, it appears that I assume Love to be a body. Concerning him I also mention that he laughed and also that he spoke—acts that are characteristic of man, especially that of laughing; therefore, it is evident that I assume Love to be human. So that this discussion may be clarified suitably for my purpose, it must first be understood that in ancient times there were no love poets* writing in the vernacular, there were only certain love poets writing in Latin; and, among us, let me say (and this probably happened in other nations as it still happens in the case of Greece) it was not vernacular poets but lettered poets who dealt with these things. Not many years have passed since these vernacular poets first appeared and I call them 'poets' for to compose verse in the vernacular is more or less the same as composing classical metres in Latin.* And proof that it is but a short time is the fact that if we look into the Provençal and the Italian literatures,* we will not find poems written more than one hundred and fifty years before the present time. The reason why a few thick-witted poets acquired the fame of knowing how to compose is that they were, in a manner of speaking, the first who wrote in the Italian language. The first to begin writing as a vernacular poet was moved to do so by a desire to make his words understandable to ladies who found Latin verses difficult to comprehend. And this is an argument against those who compose in the vernacular on a subject other than love,* since such a manner of writing was from the beginning invented for the treating of love. We can conclude then, since, in Latin, greater poetic licence is conceded to the poet than to the prose writer, and since these Italian poets are nothing more than poets writing in the vernacular, that it is fitting and reasonable that greater licence be granted them than to other writers in the vernacular; therefore, if any image or colouring of words is conceded to the Latin poets, it should be conceded to the Italian poet. So, if we discover that the Latin poets have spoken to inanimate objects as if they possessed sense and reason and have made them speak to each other, and that they did this not only with real things but also with unreal things (that is to say: they have said, concerning things that do not exist, that they speak, and they have said that many an accident in substance speaks as if it were a substance and human), then it is fitting that the vernacular poet do the same, not without some reason but rather with a motive that later can be revealed by prose. That the Latin poets have spoken in the manner I have just described can be seen through Virgil, who says that Juno, a goddess hostile to the Trojans, spoke to Aeolus, god of the winds, here in the first book of the *Aeneid*: 'Aeolus, for to you', and that this god answered her: 'Yours, O queen, is the task of determining your wishes; mine is the right to obey orders.'* For this same poet inanimate things speak to animate things here in the third book of the *Aeneid*: 'You hardy Trojans.'* In Lucan the animate object speaks to the inanimate object, here: 'Much, Rome, do you nevertheless owe to civic arms.'* In Horace a man speaks to his own intelligence as if to another person, and not only are they the words of Horace but he says them virtually quoting the good Homer, in this passage of *The Art of Poetry*: 'Tell me, Muse, of the man.'* In Ovid, Love speaks as if he were a human being in the beginning of the book called *The Remedy of Love*: 'Wars against me I see,

wars are preparing, he says.'* From the foregoing explanation anyone who experiences difficulties in certain parts of
this, my little book, can find a solution for them. And in
order that some thick-witted person not become too daring
from what I have said, let me add that just as the Latin
poets did not write as they did without a reason, so vernacular poets should not write in the same way without having
some reason for writing as they do; for great embarrassment
would come to one who, having written things in the dress
of an image or rhetorical colouring, and then, having been
asked, would not be able to strip his words of such dress
in order to give them their true meaning.* And my first
friend and I are well acquainted with some who compose
so witlessly.

XXVI

THIS most gracious lady of whom I have spoken in the preceding poems came into such widespread favour among the people that when she walked down a street, people ran to see her. This gave me the greatest joy. And when she was near someone, such modesty filled that one's heart that he dared neither to raise his eyes nor to return her greeting; and many, having experienced this, could testify to it for whoever might not believe. Crowned with and clothed in humility, she would go her way, showing no airs of superiority because of what she heard and saw. Many said after she had passed by: 'This is no woman, but rather one of heaven's most beautiful angels.' And others would say: 'This is a miracle; blessed be the Lord who works so miraculously.' I say that she displayed such decorum and was so filled with every charm that those who gazed at her experienced within themselves a pure and sweet delight, such that they were unable to describe it; nor was there anyone who could gaze at her without immediately having to sigh. These and still more marvellous things emanated powerfully from her; wherefore, thinking of this and desiring to resume the theme of her praise, I decided to write words in which I would explain her praiseworthy and beneficent influences so that not only those who could see her with their eyes but others as well might know of her whatever words can express. Therefore I wrote this sonnet, which begins: 'Such sweet decorum'.*

> Such sweet decorum and such gentle graces
>   attend my lady's greeting as she walks
>   that every tongue is stammering then mute,
> and eyes dare not to gaze at such a sight;
> she moves benignly in humility
> untouched by all the praise along her way

and seems a creature come from heaven to earth,
a miracle manifest in reality.
So charming she appears to human sight,
her sweetness through the eyes reaches the heart;
who has not felt this cannot understand.
And from her lips it seems there moves a spirit
so gentle and so loving that it glides
into the souls of men and whispers, 'Sigh!'

This sonnet is so easy to understand from what has preceded it that it has no need of division; therefore, leaving it, I say that my lady* came into such high favour that not only was she honoured and praised but also many other ladies were honoured and praised through her. Seeing this and wishing to make it evident to those who did not see it, I decided to write more words in which this would be brought out. And then I wrote this next sonnet, which begins, 'He sees an affluence', telling how her virtuous power worked on others, as is shown in the division.

He sees an affluence of joy ideal
who sees my lady where the others are;
all those who keep her company must give
their thanks to God for such sweet grace as this.
Her beauty has such influence on them
that it does not provoke another's envy,
but rather makes them want to be like her,
to move in love and faith and graciousness.
Her face gives meekness to each thing it sees
and makes not only her beatified,
but adds its praise to everyone around her.
So gracious is each gesture that she makes
that no one can recall her to his mind
and not sigh in an ecstasy of love.

This sonnet has three parts. In the first I tell among what people this lady appeared most admirable; in the second I tell how gracious was her company; in the third I tell of those things which she miraculously brought about in others. The second part begins with the words: 'all those'; the third with: 'Her beauty'. This last part divides into three: in the first I tell what she wrought in ladies, through the effect produced in them; in the second I tell what she did for them through the eyes of others; in the third I tell how she miraculously affects not only ladies but all persons and not only while in her presence but also when recalling her to mind. The second begins with the words: 'Her face'; the third with: 'So gracious'.

XXVII

SOMETIME after this I began one day thinking over what I had said about my lady in these two preceding sonnets, and considering that I had not mentioned anything about the effect she had on me at the present time, I decided that I had spoken insufficiently. Therefore I made up my mind to write something in which I would tell how I am disposed to her influence and how her miraculous power worked in me; and believing I would not be able to tell this in the short space of a sonnet, I immediately began a *canzone**
which starts: 'So long a time'.

So long a time has Love kept me a slave
   and in his lordship fully seasoned me,
   that even though at first I felt him harsh,
   now tender is his power in my heart.
   But when he takes my strength away from me
   so that my spirits seem to run away,
   my fainting soul is overcome with sweetness
   and the colour of my face begins to fade.
Then in me Love starts working up such power,
   he makes my spirits rant and wander off,
   and rushing out they call
   my lady, begging her to grant me grace.
   This happens every time she looks at me;
   I am more humbled than my words can tell.

XXVIII

'HOW doth the city sit solitary that was full of people! How is she become a widow, she that was great among the nations!'* I was still involved in composing this *canzone*, and I had completed the above stanza when the God of Justice called this most gracious one to glory under the banner of the Blessed Virgin Mary, whose name was always spoken with the greatest reverence by the blessed Beatrice. And even though I would like to discuss somewhat her departure from us, it is not my intention to do so here for three reasons. The first is that it was not intended to be included, if we consider the preface at the beginning of this little book; the second is that even if it had been my intention, the language at my command at this time would not suffice to deal with the material in the way it should be dealt with; the third is that even supposing the first and the second reasons did not exist, it still would not be proper for me to deal with it since dealing with it would entail praising myself, a thing exceedingly blameworthy in the one who does it. Therefore I leave such a topic to some other writer. Nevertheless, since the number nine has appeared many times among the preceding words, which clearly could not happen without a reason, and since in her departure this number obviously played a large role, I think it fitting that I say something here concerning this, inasmuch as it seems pertinent to my theme. And so I shall tell first about the part it played in her departure, and then I shall give some reasons why this number was so close to her.

XXIX

I WILL begin by saying that if one counts in the Arabian fashion,* her most worthy soul departed during the first hour of the ninth day of the month, and if one reckons in the Syrian manner, she departed in the ninth month of the year, the first month there being Tixryn the First,* which for us is October. And according to our reckoning she departed in that year of our Christian era, that is in the year of Our Lord, in which the perfect number had been completed for the ninth time* in that century in which she had been placed in this world: she was a Christian of the thirteenth century. Another reason why this number was in such harmony with her might be this: since according to Ptolemy as well as according to Christian truth there are nine heavens that move, and since according to widespread astrological opinion these heavens affect the earth below following the relation they have to one another, this number was well disposed to her in order to make it understood that at her birth all nine of the moving heavens* were in perfect relationship* to one another. This is just one reason for it; but in more subtle thinking and according to the infallible truth, she and this number are actually synonymous; that is, through analogy. What I mean to say is this: the number three is the root of nine, for without any other number, multiplied by itself it gives nine, as we plainly see that three times three is nine. Therefore, if three is the sole factor of nine and the sole factor of miracles is three, that is, Father, Son, and Holy Ghost, who are three in One, then this lady is accompanied by the number nine so that it may be understood that she was a nine, or a miracle, whose root, namely of the miracle, is the miraculous Trinity itself. Perhaps a more subtle person would see in this still another more subtle explanation, but this is the one that I see and that pleases me the most.

XXX

AFTER she had departed from this world, all of the previously mentioned city remained as a widow stripped of all dignity; and I, still weeping in this barren city,* wrote to the princes of the land concerning its condition, taking my beginning from the prophet Jeremiah where he says: 'How doth the city sit solitary'.* And I say this so that no one will wonder why I cited these words above: it was to serve as a preface for the new material that follows. And if someone should wish to reproach me for the fact that I do not include here the words which follow those already quoted, my excuse is this: since it was my intention from the beginning to write in the vernacular, and since the words which follow those quoted are all in Latin,* it would be contrary to my intention if I were to write them. And I know that my best friend,* for whom I write this, has the same intention; namely, that I should write entirely in the vernacular.

XXXI

AFTER my eyes had wept for some time and were so wept out that they could no longer relieve my sadness, I thought of trying to relieve it with some doleful words; whereupon I decided to compose a *canzone* in which, weeping, I would speak of her through whom so much grief had become the destroyer of my soul. Then I began to write a *canzone* which begins: 'The eyes grieving'. And in order that this *canzone* may appear to remain more widow-like after its completion, I shall divide it before I write it, and I shall follow this method from now on.

Let me say that this sad little song has three parts. The first is introductory; in the second I speak of her; in the third I speak beseechingly to the *canzone*. The second part begins with the words 'Beatrice has ascended', the third with 'Now go your way'. The first part breaks down into three. In the first I say why I am moved to speak; in the second I tell to whom it is I wish to speak; in the third I tell who it is I wish to speak about. The second begins here: 'Since I remember'; the third here: 'And then lamenting'. Then when I say, 'Beatrice has ascended', I am speaking about her, and of this I make two parts. First I tell the reason why she was taken from us; then I tell how some lament her departure, and I begin this part with the words: 'And once removed'. This part further divides into three. In the first I mention who does not weep for her; in the second I mention who does weep for her; in the third I tell of my own condition. The second begins: 'But sadness'; the third: 'Weeping and pain'. Then when I say, 'Now go your way', I am speaking to this *canzone*, designating the ladies to whom it is to go and with whom it is to remain.

> The eyes grieving through pity for the heart
> while weeping have endured great suffering

so that they are defeated, tearless eyes.
And now if I should want to vent that grief,
which gradually leads me to my death,
I must express myself in anguished words.
Since I remember how I loved to speak
about my lady when she was alive,
addressing, gracious ladies, you alone;
I will not speak to others
but only to a lady's tender heart.
And then lamenting, I shall tell them how
she suddenly ascended into heaven
and how she left Love here to grieve with me.
Beatrice has ascended to high heaven,
into a realm where angels live in peace;
she dwells with them, and you she leaves behind
The coldness did not take her from the earth
nor was it heat, as is the fate of others;
it was her great unselfishness alone.
Because the light of her humility
cut through the heavens with such forcefulness,
it even made the Lord Eternal marvel;
and then a sweet desire
moved Him to summon up such blessedness,
and from down here he had her brought to Him
because He saw that our offensive life
did not deserve so decorous a thing.
And once removed from its enchanting form,
the tender soul, perfectly filled with grace,*
now lives with glory in a worthy place.
Who speaks of her and does not weeping speak,
possesses heart of stone so hard and vile
no kindly sentiment could penetrate.
No evil heart could have sufficient wit
to conceive in any way what she was like,
and so it has no urge to weep from grief.
But sadness and desire come
to sigh and then to die a death of tears,
and consolation from the soul is stripped
in anyone who pictures in his thoughts
what she was like and how she went from us.

The power of my sighs fills me with anguish
   each time the thought brings to my weary mind
   the image of that one who split my heart;
   and many times while contemplating death,
   so sweet an urge to die comes over me
   it drains away the colour from my face.
   When this imagining has hold of me,
   bitter affliction bounds me on all sides,
   and I begin to tremble from the pain;
   then I become so changed
   that shame drives me away from everyone
   then weeping, all alone in my distress,
   I call to Beatrice, 'Can you be dead?'
   And but to call on her restores my soul.
Weeping and pain and many an anguished sigh
   torment my heart each time I am alone.
   Should someone hear me, he as well would grieve;
   and what my life has been since she I loved
   took leave of earth and went to the new realm
   there is not any tongue could tell of it.
   And so, my ladies, even if I tried,
   I could not tell you what I have become,
   so does my bitter life entangle me,
   a life so much abased
   that every man who sees my fading face
   it seems cries out to me, 'I cast you out.'
   But what I am my lady can perceive,
   and I still hope that she will show me grace.
Now go your way in tears, sad little song,
   and find once more the ladies and the maidens
   to whom your sister poems*
   were wont to be the messengers of joy;
   and you who are the daughter of despair,
   go now disconsolate, and stay with them.

XXXII

AFTER this *canzone* was composed a person came to me
who, according to degrees of friendship, was second after my
first friend.* And he was so closely related to this glorious
lady that he could not have been any closer. After he had
spoken with me awhile, he requested I write something for
him about a lady who was dead; and he disguised his words
in such a way as to appear to speak of a different person
who had recently died. But I, being aware that he could be
speaking only about that blessed one, told him I would do
as he asked. Then thinking it over, I decided to compose a
sonnet which would be sent to this friend of mine, in which
I would express my sorrow in such a way that it would seem
to be his. Then I wrote this sonnet, which begins with the
words, 'Now come to me', and it consists of two parts. In
the first part I call upon Love's faithful to listen to me; in
the second I tell about my wretched condition. The second
part begins here: 'the sighs that issue'.

> Now come to me and listen to my sighs,
>   O gracious hearts, for pity wants it so,
>   the sighs that issue in despondency.
>   But for their help I would have died of grief,
>   because my eyes would be in debt to me,
>   owing much more than they could hope to pay
>   by weeping for my lady in such way
>   that mourning her, my heart might be relieved.
> And ceaselessly shall sighs of mine be heard
>   calling upon my lady, who is gone
>   to dwell where worth like hers is merited,
>   and heard the sighs of scorn for this our life,
>   as if they were the mournful soul itself
>   abandoned by its hope of happiness.

XXXIII

AFTER I had composed this sonnet, thinking of the person to whom I intended to give it as if written by him, I realized that the favour seemed poor and empty for a person so closely related to this glorious lady. Therefore, before I gave him the above-written sonnet, I wrote two stanzas of a *canzone*, one of them truly on behalf of my friend and the other on my own, although to one who does not observe carefully, they both appear to speak for the same person. But he who examines them closely sees clearly that different people are speaking, since one does not call her his lady while the other does, as is clearly shown. I gave him this *canzone* and the above-written sonnet telling him that I had written it all on his behalf.

This *canzone* begins, 'Whenever I recall', and it has two parts. In the first, that is, the first stanza, this friend of mine and close relative of hers laments; in the second I myself lament, that is, in the other stanza which begins: 'And there is blended'. And in this fashion it is evident that in this *canzone* two people are lamenting, one of whom grieves as a brother, the other as Love's servant.

> Whenever I recall to mind, oh grief!
>   that I shall nevermore
>   behold the lady that I ever mourn,
>   such agony is packed around my heart
>   by my pained memory,
>   it makes me say: 'My soul, why don't you leave?
>   The torments you will have to suffer here
>   upon this earth, which even now you hate,
>   weigh heavily upon my fearful mind.'
>   Then calling upon death,
>   as I would call on lovely, soothing peace,
>   I say, with love so yearning, 'Come to me,'

that I am jealous of whoever dies.
And there is blended out of all my sighs
  a chorus of beseeching
  that constantly keeps calling upon death.
  Towards this has turned each one of my desires
  since that day when my lady
  was taken from me by death's cruelty.
  This is because the pleasure of her beauty,
  having removed itself from mortal sight,
    was transformed into beauty of the soul
    spreading throughout the heavens
    a light of love that greets the angels there,
    and moves their keen and lofty intellects
    to marvel at such graciousness as hers.

XXXIV

ON that day which completed one year since this lady had become a citizen of the eternal life, I was sitting in a place where, thinking of her, I was drawing an angel on some panels.* And while I was drawing, I turned my head and saw alongside me some men* to whom all consideration was due. They were looking at what I was doing, and, as I was later told, they had already been there some time before I became aware of it. When I saw them, I stood up and greeting them said: 'Someone was with me just now; that is why I was so deep in thought.' When they left, I returned to my work of drawing figures of angels, and while I was doing this a thought came to me to write some poetry in the form of an anniversary poem, and to address it to those men who had come to me. And so I wrote this sonnet which begins 'The gracious lady', and which has two beginnings; and for this reason I divide it according to the one and then according to the other.

Now, following the first beginning, this sonnet has three parts. In the first I mention that this lady was already in my mind; in the second I tell what Love therefore did to me; in the third I tell of the effects of Love. The second begins: 'Love, who perceived'; the third: 'Lamenting, they'. This last part divides into two. In the first I tell that all my sighs came forth speaking; in the second I tell how some spoke different words from the others. The second begins here: 'but those'. Following the other beginning, this sonnet divides in the same way, except that in the first part I mention at what moment this lady had come into my memory as she did, and this I do not mention in the other.

First beginning
The gracious lady came into my mind,
    the lady who because of her great worth
    was placed by his most lofty Majesty

in that calm realm of heaven where Mary is.

Second beginning

That gracious lady came into my mind,
    that lady for whom Love is weeping still,
    the moment you were called here by her power
    that drew you here to see what I was doing.
    Love, who perceived her in my memory,
    had come awake within the ravaged heart
    and to my sighs he said, 'Go forth from here,'
    whereat each one went on his grieving way.
Lamenting, they came pouring from my heart,
    together in a single voice that often
    brings painful tears into my grieving eyes;
    but those that pour forth with the greatest pain
    were saying: 'Today, O intellect sublime,
    completes a year since you went up to heaven.'

XXXV

SOMETIME afterward, because I happened to be in a place which recalled past times, I was very pensive and full of thoughts so doleful that they must have given my face a look of terrifying distress. And so, becoming aware of my disturbed condition, I raised my eyes to see whether anyone was looking at me. And I saw a gracious lady,* young and very beautiful, who was at a window looking down at me so compassionately, to judge by her appearance, that it seemed all pity was concentrated in her. And since it is true that whenever a miserable person sees someone who has compassion for him, he is the more readily moved to tears, as if taking pity on himself, so I then felt the tears start to come. Fearing that I was displaying my degraded state, I departed from beneath the eyes of this gracious one, and lat er on I said to myself: 'It cannot help but be that in company with that compassionate lady there is most noble Love.' Thereupon I decided to write a sonnet in which I would address her and would include in it all that I have narrated in this account.* And since through this account it is sufficiently clear, I shall not analyse it. The sonnet begins: 'My eyes have seen'.

> My eyes have seen how much of Pity's look
>   displayed itself upon your countenance
>   when you observed the bearing and the mien
>   which often I am forced by grief to show.
> Then I became aware that you had seen
>   into the nature of my darkened life,
>   and this aroused within my heart a fear
>   of showing through my eyes my wretched state.
> I fled then from your presence as I felt
>   the tears begin to overflow my heart
>   that at the sight of you was overwhelmed.
>   Later within my anguished soul I said:

'For certain with that lady dwells that Love
that makes me go about like this in tears.'

XXXVI

AFTERWARDS it happened that wherever this lady saw me, her face became compassionate and of a pale colour almost like that of love, so that many times I was reminded of my most worthy lady who always displayed a similar colour. And often when I was unable to weep or to vent my sadness, I used to go to see this compassionate lady, whose appearance alone was able to fill my eyes with tears. And therefore the urge came to me to write some poetry addressed to her, and I wrote this sonnet, which begins: 'Colour of Love'. And because of the foregoing account, it is clear without analysis.

Colour of Love and air of sympathy
   have never so miraculously seized
   the face of any lady when she gazed
   at eyes susceptible of anguished tears,
   as they seized yours whenever you beheld
   arriving in your presence my sad face;
      and so through you a thought comes to my mind,
      such that I greatly fear my heart will split.
I cannot keep my devastated eyes
   from looking ever and again at you
   because of their desire to shed tears;
   and you intensify their longing so
   that by this yearning they are all consumed,
   for in your presence they cannot weep tears.

XXXVII

THE sight of this lady brought me to the point that my
eyes began to delight too much in seeing her; I often became
angry with myself about it, and I felt very contemptible
indeed. As a result, many times I would curse the wantonness of my eyes, and in my thoughts I would say to them:
'You used to make all those who saw your sad state weep,
and now it seems that you wish to forget all that because
of this lady who gazes at you and who does so only to grieve
for the glorious lady for whom you used to mourn. Do as
you please, but I shall remind you of her many times,
damned eyes, for never, except after death, should your tears
have ceased.' And after I had said this to myself addressing
my eyes, deep and anguished sighs assailed me. And so that
this conflict that I was having with myself should not remain
known solely to the wretch that experienced it, I decided
to compose a sonnet and to express in it this dreadful
condition. And I wrote this sonnet, which begins 'The bitter
tears', and it has two parts. In the first I speak to my eyes
the way my heart was speaking within me; in the second I
prevent any ambiguity by making clear who it is that speaks
this way, and this part begins here: 'So says my heart'.
It could very well receive still further analysis, but this
would be superfluous since the preceding account makes its
meaning clear.

> 'The bitter tears that have been shed by you,
>   O eyes of mine, and for so long a time,
>   have made the tears of other persons flow
>   for pity's sake, as you yourselves have seen.
>   And now it seems to me you would forget,
>   if I were so disloyal, for my part,
>   as not to take from you all chance of it,
>   recalling to you her whom once you wept.

Your infidelity fills me with care;
   it frightens me, and I have come to dread
   the lady's face that often looks on you.
   Never should you, until death takes your sight,
   forget our gracious lady who is dead.'
So says my heart and afterwards it sighs.

XXXVIII

THE appearance of this lady brought about in me such a strange condition that often I would reason as one does who is infatuated. I thought of her in this way: 'This is a lady, gracious, beautiful, young, and prudent, and perhaps she has appeared through the will of Love in order that my life may know some peace.' And many times I thought more lovingly, so much so that the heart consented to it, that is to the loving thought. And when I had consented to this, I reconsidered as if moved by reason, and I said to myself: 'Lord, what kind of thought is this that tries to console me in such base fashion and practically leaves me no other thought?' Then another thought rose up and said to me: 'Now that you have suffered such tribulation, why do you not want to escape from so much bitterness? You see that this is an inspiration of Love, which brings loving thoughts into our presence, and it proceeds from so gracious a source as the eyes of the lady who has shown us so much compassion.' Wherefore I, having battled like this within myself so many times, wished to write more poetry about it, and since in the battle of the thoughts those won who spoke in the lady's favour, it seemed to me it would be fitting to address myself to her. And I wrote this sonnet, which begins, 'A gracious thought', and I say 'gracious' inasmuch as it had a gracious lady for its subject, for in all other respects it was most base.

In this sonnet I make two parts of myself in accordance with the way in which my thoughts were divided. One I call *heart*, that is desire; the other *soul*, that is reason; and I relate what one says to the other. And that to call desire *heart* and reason *soul* is justifiable is entirely evident to those to whom I want it to be evident. True it is that in the preceding sonnet I take the part of the heart against the eyes, and this seems contrary to what I am saying in the present one. Therefore let me state that there, too, the heart stands for desire, since my greatest desire was still that of remembering my most gracious lady rather than gazing at this one, even though I did have some desire for her then; but it seemed slight. And so it is evident that one interpretation is not contrary to the other.

This sonnet has three parts. In the first I begin to tell this lady how my desire turns completely toward her; in the second I tell how the soul, meaning reason, speaks to the heart, meaning the desire; in the third I tell how the latter replies. The second part begins: 'The soul says'; the third: 'The heart replies'.

A gracious thought, because it speaks of you,
    comes frequently to dwell awhile with me,
    and so melodiously speaks of love,
    it talks the heart into surrendering.
    The soul says to the heart: 'Who is this one
    that comes with consolation for our mind
    and who, possessing such outrageous strength,
    will not allow another thought to stay?'
The heart replies: 'O reasonable soul,
    this is a tender and new spirit of Love,
    who brings all his desires here to me;
    his very life and all of his intensity
    have come from that compassionate one's eyes
    who worried so about our martyrdom.'

XXXIX

ONE day about the hour of nones* there arose in me
against this adversary of reason a strong vision in which
I seemed to see that glorious Beatrice in those crimson
garments with which she first appeared to my eyes, and
she seemed young, of the same age as when I first
saw her. Then I began to think about her, and remembering her in the sequence of past times, my heart began
remorsefully to repent of the desire by which it had so
unworthily let itself be possessed for some time contrary to firm reason; and once I had rejected this evil desire,
all my thoughts turned back to their most gracious Beatrice.

Let me say that from then on I began to think of her so
entirely with all my shameful heart that my many sighs were
proof of it, for almost all of them while issuing forth would
exclaim what was said in my heart, that is, the name of that
most gracious one and how she departed from us. And many
times it happened that some thoughts were so filled with
anguish that I would forget both what I was thinking and
where I was. Through this rekindling of sighs, the tears
which had been soothed were started again, so that my eyes
seemed to be two things desirous only of weeping. And
often it happened that through long persistence of weeping
there developed around them a purple colour, such as often
appears in one who has endured affliction. In this way they
were justly rewarded for their wantonness, and from then
on they could not gaze at anyone who might look back at
them in such a way as to encourage again a similar inclina-
tion. And so that it be known that such evil desire and
empty temptation had been destroyed, and so that the poetry
I had written before would raise no questions, I decided to
write a sonnet which would include the essence of what I
have just related. And then I wrote: 'Alas! by the full force',

and I said 'Alas' because I was ashamed of the fact that my eyes had wandered so. I do not divide this sonnet, since its story makes it clear enough.

Alas! by the full force of many sighs
    born of the thoughts that are within my heart,
    the eyes are overcome and have no strength
    to gaze at anyone who looks at them.
    They have become what seems like twin desires,
    the one to weep, the other to show pain,
    and many times they mourn so much that Love
    encircles them with martyrdom's red crown.*
These meditations and the sighs I breathe
    become so torturing within the heart
    that Love, who dwells there, faints from so much pain;
    for they have on themselves, these grieving ones,
    the sweet name of my lady superscribed,
    and many words relating to her death.

XL

AFTER this time of tribulation,* during that season when many people go to see the blessed image that Jesus Christ left us* as a copy of His most beautiful face (which my lady beholds in glory), it happened that some pilgrims were going down a street which is near the middle of the city where* the most gracious lady was born, lived, and died. These pilgrims, it seemed to me, were going along very pensive; and I, thinking of them, said to myself: 'These pilgrims seem to come from distant parts, and I do not believe that they have ever heard mention of this lady; they know nothing about her, but rather their thoughts are of other things than these; perhaps they are thinking of their friends far away, whom we do not know.' Then I said to myself: 'I know that if they were from a neighbouring town they would in some way appear distressed while passing through the centre of the mournful city.' Again I said to myself: 'If I could detain them awhile, I certainly would make them weep before they left this city, for I could speak words that would make anyone listening to them weep.' Then after these people had passed from my sight, I decided to compose a sonnet in which I would reveal what I had said to myself. And to make it appear more pathetic, I decided to write it as if I had spoken to them, and I composed this sonnet, which begins: 'Ah pilgrims'. And I used the term 'pilgrims' according to the broad meaning of the word, for pilgrims can be understood in two ways, one general and the other specific. In the general sense a pilgrim is anyone who is out of his own country; in a specific sense 'pilgrim' means only one who travels to or returns from the house of St James.* And it is to be known further that there are three ways by which the people who travel in the service of the Most High may be accurately called. They are called *palmers* who journey across the sea to that Holy Land, whence they often bring back palms; they are called *pilgrims* who journey to the house of Galicia, because the tomb of St James is farther away from his own country than that of any other apostle; they are called *romers* who travel to Rome, where these whom I call *pilgrims* were going.

I do not analyse this sonnet since its story makes it clear enough.

> Ah pilgrims, moving pensively along,
>   thinking perhaps of things that are not here,
>   do you travel from towns as far away
>   as your appearance would make us believe?
>   You do not weep as you are passing through
>   the middle of the city in its grief;
>   you act like those who do not understand
>   a thing about its grievous weight of woe.
> If you would stop to listen to me speak,
>   I know, from what my sighing heart is saying,
>   that afterwards you will depart in tears:
>   Lost is the city's source of blessedness,
>   and words that one can say concerning her
>   have power to bring any man to tears.

XLI

SOME time afterwards two worthy ladies sent word to me requesting that I send them some poetry of mine. Taking into consideration their worthiness, I decided to send them some poems and to write something new to send along with them—in this way I would fulfil their request with more honour. So I wrote this sonnet which tells of my condition, and I sent it to them accompanied by the preceding sonnet and by another one which begins: 'Now come to me and listen'.*

The new sonnet I wrote begins 'Beyond the sphere',* and contains five parts. In the first I tell where my thought is going, naming it after one of its effects. In the second I tell why it goes up there, that is, who causes it to go. In the third I tell what it saw, that is a lady being honoured up there, and I call it a 'pilgrim spirit' because it makes the journey up there spiritually and once there it is like a pilgrim far from home. In the fourth I tell how it sees her to be such, that is of such a nature, that I cannot understand it: that is to say that my thought ascends into the nature of this lady to such a degree that my mind cannot grasp it, for our mind functions in relation to those blessed souls as the weak eye does in relation to the sun, and this the Philosopher tells us in the second book of the *Metaphysics.** In the fifth part I say that even though I cannot understand what my thought has taken me to see, that is her miraculous nature, at least I understand this much: this thought of mine is entirely about my lady, for many times I hear her name in my thought. At the end of this fifth part I say, 'dear ladies', to make it understood that it is to ladies that I speak. The second part begins: 'a strange, new understanding'; the third part: 'When it has reached'; the fourth: 'But when'; the fifth: 'this much'. One could divide it and explain it more subtly, but since it can pass with this analysis, I do not concern myself with further division.

Beyond the sphere that makes the widest round,
   passes the sigh which issues from my heart;
   a strange, new understanding that sad Love
   imparts to it keeps urging it on high.
   When it has reached the place of its desiring,
   it sees a lady held in reverence,
   splendid in light, and through her radiance
   the pilgrim spirit gazes at her being.
But when it tries to tell me what it saw,
   I cannot understand the subtle words
   it speaks to the sad heart that makes it speak.
   I know it talks of that most gracious one,
   because it often mentions Beatrice;
   this much is very clear to me, dear ladies.

XLII

AFTER this sonnet there appeared to me a miraculous vision in which I saw things that made me resolve to say no more about this blessed one until I would be capable of writing about her in a more worthy fashion. And to achieve this I am striving as hard as I can, and this she truly knows. Accordingly, if it be the wish of Him through whom all things flourish that my life continue for a few more years, I hope to write of her* that which has never been written of any other woman. And then may it please that One who is the Lord of Graciousness that my soul ascend to behold the glory of its lady, that is, of that blessed Beatrice, who in glory gazes upon the countenance of the One *who is through all ages blessed.**

EXPLANATORY NOTES

3   '*Here begins a new life*': appearing in the text in Latin: 'Incipit vita nova'.

4   *heaven of light*: the Sun; the fourth heaven of the Universe in the Ptolemaic system. Radiating in concentric circles from the centre Earth were the Moon, Mercury, Venus, Sun, Mars, Jupiter, Saturn, the Fixed Stars, the Primum Mobile, and the Empyrean.

    twelfth of a degree: the Fixed Stars (the eighth heaven) were believed to move from west to east one degree in 100 years (or one-twelfth of a degree in eight years and four months), a phenomenon known now as precession of the equinoxes.

    vital spirit: in this passage Dante mentions the three physiological spirits, the vital, the animal, and the natural, taking his categories from Albertus Magnus (*De Spiritu et Respiratione*). These spirits had substance; the vital originating in the heart, becoming natural in the liver, and animal in the brain. They were all three ruled by the soul.

    '*Here is a god . . . over me*': appearing in the text in Latin: 'Ecce deus fortior me, qui veniens dominabitur michi.'

    spirits of sight: one of the *spiriti sensitivi*, emanations of the *spirito animale* that act as vehicles for the senses. The spirits of sight travelled to the object and back to the eyes, carrying the image.

    '*Now your bliss has appeared*': cited in Latin: 'Apparuit iam beatitudo vestra.'

    '*Alas, wretch . . . often*': in Latin in the text: 'Heu miser, quia frequenter impeditus ero deinceps!'

5   '*She did not seem . . . a god*': these words, however, appear in Italian; an allusion to the *Iliad*, xxiv. 258–9 (regarding Hector), which Dante knew from his reading of Aristotle. Homer had not yet been translated into Latin, and Dante did not know Greek.

5 *ninth hour*: the canonical hours of the day began at six in
   the morning.

   marvellous vision: the first of three visions in the *Vita
   nuova*. Cf. Ezekiel 1–3.

   '*I am your master*': in Latin in the text: 'Ego dominus tuus.'

   '*Behold your heart*': in Latin in the text: 'Vide cor tuum.'

7 *fourth hour of the night*: the hours of the night began at 6
   p.m. It was between 9 and 10 p.m.

   famous poets: lyric poets accustomed to debate problems of
   love in verse.

   began this sonnet: the Italian troubadours invented the
   sonnet form, still a mode of debate in which the problem
   is set forth in a *proposta*, inviting a *risposta* (using the same
   rhymes) from another poet. Together the two sonnets
   formed a *tenzone*.

   sweet lord's sake: Love is the powerful lord whom the poets
   serve as subjects.

   my first friend: the poet Guido Cavalcanti (1259?–1300),
   who died in exile after banishment by Dante's own party
   and with his consent. Cf. *Inferno*, x. 58–111; *Purgatorio*,
   xi. 97.

8 *keep secret*: the identity of his beloved.

9 *queen of glory*: the Virgin Mary.

   a screen for the truth: this pretended devotion to another
   woman was a common device of the troubadour poets.

10 *serventese*: the *sirventes* in Provençal poetry was a political
   poem; in Italy it became narrative, often characterizing
   individuals in a critical or satiric manner. No trace of
   Dante's *serventese* has been found.

11 *this sonnet*: this is a *sonetto doppio* (or *rinterzato*) in which
   six 7-syllable lines are inserted among the usual 11-syllable
   lines, each rhyming with the line preceding. Another *sonetto
   doppio* appears in Chapter VIII.

   O you . . . mine: these lines paraphrase Lamentations of
   Jeremiah 1: 12, which Dante quotes in the prose at the end
   of the sonnet.

12   *'All ye . . . sorrow'*: cited in Latin: 'O vos omnes qui tran-
sitis per viam, attendite et videte si est dolor sicut dolor
meus.'

13   *midst of many ladies*: in Boccaccio's Introduction to the
Decameron he tells of the Florentine custom of male mour-
ners remaining outside the house of a person who had died
while the females assembled inside, also keeping separate
on their way to the church.

     save sweet chastity: her honour preserved in the minds of men.

14   *Brute death*: another *sonetto doppio* with the rhyme scheme
AaBBbA.

15   *took the shape in my mind of a pilgrim*: a traveller who has
left his proper home behind.

     beautiful stream: perhaps the Arno, the river that flows
through Florence.

16   *I bring it back*: this conceit of carrying the heart about is
conventional and suggests that Dante finished one love
affair and began another while on this journey away from
Florence.

18   *drive out . . . spirits of sight*: for these spirits, see notes to
Chapter II, on pp. 1A and 2.

19   *lady of courtesy*: the Virgin Mary.

     'My son . . . pretences': cited in Latin: 'Fili mi, tempus est
ut pretermictantur simulacra nostra.'

     'I am like the centre . . . you are not': in Latin: 'Ego tam-
quam centrum circuli, cui simili modo se habent circumferentie partes, tu autem non sic.'

20   *ballad*: the *ballata* was poetry set to music, meant to be
sung during dance. It begins with a *ripresa* to be repeated
as a refrain, followed by one or more stanzas whose last
lines rhyme with one of the lines of the *ripresa*.

22   *let him understand*: he invites the reader to hold this passage
in mind until he comes to the explanation in Chapter
XXV. Cf. *Convivio*, iii. 9.

23   *'Names . . . things'*: cited in Latin: 'Nomina sunt conse-
quentia rerum'; a common gloss on civil law. Cf. Genesis
2: 19–20.

25   *the battle*: a military term, common to the troubadour lyric. Cf. 'foe' and 'defence' in Chapter XIII.

custom . . . city: weddings were regulated by the city of Florence, whose rules allowed an invited guest to bring a friend.

my spirits were so disrupted: cf. Chapters II, XI. He was unable to see Beatrice except through the eyes of Love.

26   *boundaries of life beyond which . . . return*: on the verge of the Unknown. Cf. *Inf.* xxvi. 90–142, Ulysses' account of going to his death beyond the gates of Hercules; *Hamlet*, III. i: 'The undiscovered country from whose bourn No traveller returns.'

30   *defend me in this battle*: this passage is notable for its terms of warfare, a convention for the lover being tested in his loyalty.

35   *canzone*: a poem of Provençal origin consisting of a number of stanzas identically structured. Dante considered it the noblest form of poetry and wrote of it in detail in *De Vulgari Eloquentia*, ii. It was later diversified and perfected by Petrarch. This *canzone* ('Donne ch'avete intelletto d'amore') is Dante's most famous because of its mention in *Purg.* xxiv. 49–63 as a model of the 'dolce stil novo'. This *canzone* consists of five stanzas of 14 lines, each structured like a sonnet with two quatrains and two tercets in 11-syllable verse.

36   *who when in hell . . . damned*: several interpretations of this controversial line are offered: he expects not to be saved; he anticipates the death of Beatrice and his subsequent languishing in a hell on earth without her; he anticipates his descent into hell in a future work of imagination, like the *Divine Comedy*.

paleness of the pearl, in measure suited: the colour of dawn, denoting ideal perfection in a philosophic sense.

38   *eyes . . . mouth*: the flame of desire is struck in the eyes; its goal is the mouth from which issues the greeting of the lady. Cf. *Convivio*, iii. 8.

handmaiden: the final stanza serves as messenger, technically named an *envoi*, *congedo*, or *commiato*.

38 *wit enough to understand*: professing to aim at a select
    audience was a common stance in troubadour poetry.

39 *moved to ask me*: Dante here echoes the first line of
    Cavalcanti's most famous *canzone*, 'Donna mi prega'.

    that wise poet: Guido Guinizzelli, the forerunner of Dante
    who formulated the doctrine of the gracious heart in his
    most famous *canzone* 'Al cor gentil ripara sempre Amore'.
    Guinizzelli like Dante changed his style from describing
    conventionally the sensual effects of love to exploring the
    intellectual aspects of it originating in nobility of character.
    Dante refers to Guinizzelli in *De Vulgari Eloquentia*, i. 15,
    Conv. iv. 20, *Purg*. xxvi. 97–9; he echoes this *canzone* again
    in *Inf*. v. 100.

    potential force: of *Idea*—eternal form. Cf. *Conv*. ii. 1 and
    iii. 7.

    form is to matter: cf. the Aristotelian principle of causation
    from *De anima*, ii. 2: the perfection of the thing is its
    realization in nature (entelechy) in virtue of which it
    attains its fullest function. According to Guinizzelli's
    poem, the phenomenon is like a bird finding its home and
    renewing itself in the greenness of the woods.

43 *he who had been the father*: the father of Beatrice, usually
    identified as Folco Portinari, who died in 1289 leaving six
    daughters and five sons, all of whom were mentioned in
    his will, including Beatrice.

44 *they had answered me*: the two sonnets together, question
    and answer, form a *contrasto*.

46 *the sun darken . . . earthquakes*: these phenomena are remi-
    niscent of events that accompanied the death of Christ
    (Matthew 27: 51–4; Luke 23: 44), and of Revelation 6:
    12–14.

47 *'Hosanna in the highest'*: the greeting given to Christ when
    he entered Jerusalem. Cf. Mark 11: 10; Matthew 21: 9;
    Purg. xi. 11; xx. 136.

47 *young and gracious lady*: said below to be a 'close relative',
    perhaps a younger sister.

48 *this canzone*: the longest poem in the *Vita nuova* (although
    not the longest *canzone* Dante wrote), this is the centre-

piece of the work; i.e. it is preceded by 15 poems and followed by 15 and is separated from the other two *canzoni* by four poems each. The six stanzas each have 14 lines, lines 9 and 11 being settenary. There is no *commiato*.

51 *of my first friend*: Guido Cavalcanti; cf. Chapters III, XXX. No Joan (Giovanna) has been found in the poems of Cavalcanti, although a *ballata* begins 'Fresca rosa novella, piacente Primavera'.

'I am the voice . . . Lord': in Latin in the text: 'Ego vox clamantis in deserto; parate viam Domini.' Cf. Matthew 3: 3; Mark 1: 3; Luke 3: 4; John 1: 23.

52 *Lady Bice*: the familiar name of Beatrice. A fictitious name to conceal the identity of the lady was termed a *senhal* in troubadour poetry.

53 *as if it were a thing in itself*: he speaks also of Beatrice, just identified as Love. This passage is an important example of early literary criticism.

the Philosopher: Aristotle, known to Dante through Latin translations and the writings of St Thomas Aquinas.

love poets: didactic poets who disseminated their ideas through the medium of love poetry, writing in the learned tongue.

more or less . . . classical metres in Latin: Dante argues from a Scholastic position for poetic licence in the formation of vernacular verse, composed within certain limitation. Unless writing in Latin grammar and metre, a poet technically was not called a poet.

Provençal and the Italian literatures: 'in lingua d'oco e in quella di sì'; referring to Languedoc and the Italian vernacular. Dante understood Provençal (Languedoc) to be that language spoken in southern Europe which used the Latin *hoc* for the word 'yes'. Old French (*langue d'oïl*), spoken in northern France, used *oïl* (*hoc* + *ille*). Italian used *sì* from the Latin *sic*. Cf. *Inf*. xxxiii. 80.

54 *subject other than love*: Dante later expanded his categories to include the defence of the community, virtue, and morality. Cf. *De Vulgari Eloquentia*, ii. 2.

54 '*Yours, O queen ... orders*': 'Tuus, o regina, quid optes explorare labor; michi iussa capessere fas est'; speaking of Juno (*Aeneid*, i. 65, 76–7).

'*You hardy Trojans*': 'Dardanide duri' (*Aen*. iii. 94); Phoebus is speaking in his role as the sun.

'*Much, Rome ... arms*': 'Multum, Roma, tamen debes civilibus armis' (*Pharsalia*, i. 44); addressed in the original to the Emperor.

'*Tell me ... man*': 'Dic michi, Musa, virum' (*Ars Poetica*, 141–2). In this passage, Horace translates the first two verses of Homer's *Odyssey*, making his memory of Homer's words the object of his speech.

55 '*Wars against me ... says*': 'Bella michi, video, bella parantur, ait' (*Remedia Amoris*, 2). For a mention of all four of these poets together, see *Inf*. iv. 79–90.

their true meaning: Dante invites us to find this meaning not only in his own figures or personifications but in the way they link with the figures of the four poets cited.

56 '*Such sweet decorum*': 'Tanto gentile e tanto onesta pare', Dante's most famous sonnet, in which Love's personification in Beatrice brings out her miraculous curative powers. Cf. *Conv*. iii. 7.

57 *therefore ... my lady*: some editions begin a new chapter here, adding one more to the total.

59 *a canzone*: but for one 7-syllable line (11), this poem could be a sonnet, being made up of one stanza of 14 verses. According to the *Vita nuova*'s symmetrical scheme, a sonnet is called for in this position.

60 '*How doth the city ... nations*': from the Lamentations of Jeremiah 1: 1: 'Quomodo sedet sola civitas plena populo! facta est quasi vidua domina gentium.' It is in Latin in the text.

61 *Arabian fashion*: in order to make a connection between Beatrice's death and the number nine, Dante used his knowledge of the Ptolemaic-based work *Elementa Astronomica* by Alfraganus (cf. *Conv*. ii. 5), which revealed that for Arabs, day began at sunset rather than sunrise. Beatrice died on 8 June 1290; according to the Arabian system, the first hour of the night in Italy was the first hour of 9 June.

61 *Tixryn the First*: June would be the ninth month in the Syrian system, Tixryn, a two-month period the first part of which corresponded to the Roman October.

ninth time: no foreign calendar was required to make the connection between 1290 and the number nine. It had been reached 10 times (10 being the perfect number according to St Thomas) in the thirteenth century of the Christian era.

the moving heavens: cf. *Conv.* ii. 3. In Ptolemy's system the ninth heaven is the Primum Mobile. The tenth heaven (corresponding to the perfect number) is the motionless Empyrean.

perfect relationship: as they were at the birth of Christ. Cf. *Paradiso* vi. 55–6.

62 *barren city*: Florence. By 'princes of the land' Dante may mean Florentines or he may have been addressing a wider audience. A 1314 letter addressed to the Italian cardinals meeting in Carpentras uses the same quotation from Jeremiah.

How doth the city sit solitary: in Latin in the text.

are all in Latin: Dante's letter, the first part of which is quoted in the Latin of the Vulgate (from Lamentations of Jeremiah), was all in Latin.

best friend: Guido Cavalcanti. Cf. Chapters III, XXIV. Dante implies that it was Cavalcanti who encouraged him to turn to the vernacular Italian for literary purposes. Cf. *Inf.* x. 62–3, *Conv.* i. 5–13.

64 *perfectly filled with grace*: an attribute of the Virgin Mary. Cf. Luke 1: 28; Petrarch, *canzone* 366. 40–2.

65 *your sister poems*: the other *canzoni*.

66 *second after my first friend*: believed to be the brother of Beatrice (cf. Chapter XXXIII: 'grieves as a brother').

69 *some panels*: Cennino Cennini in *Il libro dell'arte* described these *tavolette* as wooden or parchment, 6 inches square, used by beginners for exercises in drawing.

some men: men of some influence. The scene here recounted inspired Robert Browning to write the poem 'One word more' for his wife, in which these lines appear:

'Dante standing, studying his angel,—
In there broke the folk of his Inferno.
Says he—'Certain people of importance'.

71 *saw a gracious lady*: the events recounted in Chapters
XXXV–XXXIX are further treated in *Convivio*, ii, and in
the *canzone* 'Voi che 'ntendendo il terzo ciel movete'. In
Convivio, ii. 12, Dante gives an 'allegorical and true exposition' of this compassionate lady as a symbol of Philosophy. In the light of this interpretation (which follows
Dante's demonstration of her 'literal' coming into his life)
controversy has arisen about the existence of both Beatrice
and this *donna gentile* as real women. The *Convivio* pres-
umably was written some years after the *Vita nuova* when
Dante sought poetic ways to universalize his real experience, finding hidden reasons (*cagione occulto*) for what
happened, as if by 'divino imperio' (like a man who,
seeking silver, inadvertently finds gold).

in this account: in Provençal poetry such a prose account
was called 'razo', perhaps given orally when the poem or
song was recited. Boethius also alternated prose and verse
in his *Consolation of Philosophy*, a work Dante cites in
Convivio, ii, as his first investigation into philosophy.

78 *hour of nones*: ecclesiastically the period between noon and
3 p.m. (the 7th, 8th, and 9th hours of the day). Cf.
Chapters III and XII.

79 *martyrdom's red crown*: in the prose account, 'a purple
colour'.

80 *After this time of tribulation*: the exact time of the event
described here is not clear, and some commentators have
considered the chapter to be out of order, more appropri-
ately occurring soon after the death of Beatrice than after
the battle between his heart and his reason. Others date
it much later, for example in the Jubilee year 1300.

the blessed image that Jesus Christ left us: the cloth called
Veronica, imprinted with the likeness of Christ's features
when he wiped his face with it while carrying the Cross
to Calvary, preserved at St Peter's in Rome and displayed
to the faithful from time to time. Cf. *Par.* xxxi. 103–8;
Petrarch, sonnet 16.

the city where: Florence, although never named in the *Vita nuova*.

house of St James: after his death at the order of Herod (cf. Acts 12: 2) the body of the apostle James was said to have been transported miraculously to Galicia in north-western Spain. The burial place at Santiago de Compostela—pointed out by a star in the ninth century—was a frequent destination for pilgrims in the Middle Ages. Cf. *Par.* xxv. 17–18; *Conv.* ii. 14.

82 *'Now come to me and listen'*: this sonnet appears in Chapter XXXII.

'Beyond the sphere': to the Empyrean where Beatrice dwells.

Metaphysics: Aristotle's work which Dante knew from reading St Thomas Aquinas. The analogy of the eye and the sun is St Thomas's.

84 *I hope to write of her*: after a period of intense study to write of his vision of Beatrice in a more worthy manner; i.e. in the *Divine Comedy*. Cf. *Conv.* ii.

'who is through all ages blessed': in Latin in the text: 'qui est per omnia secula benedictus'.

The Oxford World's Classics Website

www.worldsclassics.co.uk

- Information about new titles
- Explore the full range of Oxford World's Classics
- Links to other literary sites and the main OUP webpage
- Imaginative competitions, with bookish prizes
- Peruse *Compass*, the Oxford World's Classics magazine
- Articles by editors
- Extracts from Introductions
- A forum for discussion and feedback on the series
- Special information for teachers and lecturers

www.worldsclassics.co.uk

American Literature

British and Irish Literature

Children's Literature

Classics and Ancient Literature

Colonial Literature

Eastern Literature

European Literature

History

Medieval Literature

Oxford English Drama

Poetry

Philosophy

Politics

Religion

The Oxford Shakespeare

A complete list of Oxford Paperbacks, including Oxford World's Classics, OPUS, Past Masters, Oxford Authors, Oxford Shakespeare, Oxford Drama, and Oxford Paperback Reference, is available in the UK from the Academic Division Publicity Department, Oxford University Press, Great Clarendon Street, Oxford OX2 6DP.

In the USA, complete lists are available from the Paperbacks Marketing Manager, Oxford University Press, 198 Madison Avenue, New York, NY 10016.

Oxford Paperbacks are available from all good bookshops. In case of difficulty, customers in the UK can order direct from Oxford University Press Bookshop, Freepost, 116 High Street, Oxford OX1 4BR, enclosing full payment. Please add 10 per cent of published price for postage and packing.